The Sundering Blade

A Thousand Li World Novel

by

Tao Wong

Copyright

This is a work of fiction. Names, characters, businesses, places, events, and incidents are either the products of the author's imagination or used in a fictitious manner. Any resemblance to actual persons, living or dead, or actual events is purely coincidental.

No part of this publication may be reproduced, distributed, or transmitted in any form or by any means, including photocopying, recording, or other electronic or mechanical methods, without the prior written permission of the publisher, except in the case of brief quotations embodied in critical reviews and certain other noncommercial uses permitted by copyright law.

The Sundering Blade

Published by Starlit Publishing
PO Box 30035
High Park PO
Toronto, ON
M6P 3K0
Canada

www.starlitpublishing.com

Ebook ISBN: 9781778551239
Paperback ISBN: 9781778551246

Books in the A Thousand Li Series

Main Series

The First Step

The First Stop

The First War

The Second Expedition

The Second Sect

The Second Storm

The Third Kingdom

The Third Realm

The Third Cut

The Fourth Stage

The Fourth Fall

The Fourth Wall

A Thousand Li World Novel

The Sundering Blade

Short Stories

The Favored Son

The Storming White Clouds Sect

On Gods and Demons

Clifftop Crisis and Transformation

Imperial March

Villages & Illnesses

Descent from the Mountain

The Divine Peak

Fish Ball Quest

Ten Thousand and One Fates

Contents

Chapter 1

The lowland lake was muddy with silt churned awake by the floods that had swept through the province days ago. In passing, it had taken villages and lives in equal measure. Stray boards and broken pieces of housing still floated through the lake, carried by the rushing water toward the clogged and teeming exit. Trees at the new shores of the overflowing body of water leaned precariously, even as the cries of cranes and ducks echoed through the deceptively peaceful surroundings.

Approaching the clogged entrance, the *hongtou*[1] slowed, the single, long sculling oar—the *yuloh*—pausing before being raised from the water. At the head of the boat, standing silently, a man regarded the exit of the lake with

---

[1] Hongtou (redhead) are sampans, which are a relatively flat-bottomed boat used mostly for rivers, lakes, and coastal waters. The hongtou often has a small shelter onboard and resembles the punting boats more familiar to Western readers.

compressed lips. He was young, barely in his mid-twenties if you could trust his features, though the expensive, black silk robes with dark green edging and the sect crest on its chest spoke of his standing as an immortal cultivator.

"Do not stop," Cheng Zhao Wan said, his voice calm and commanding and highly refined. No peasant guttural growls or the sharp hiss of the tribesmen, but a nobleman's speech.

At the back, the fisherman dipped the yuloh into the water once more.

Rather than reach for the unadorned *jian* by his side, Zhao Wan swung his right hand in a lazy cutting motion. Blade intent ripped outward, empowered by the barest fraction of chi from his *dantian,* before impacting the blockage, sending wood and water spiraling away and making the smell of mud and churning waters rise anew.

Gulping, the boatman pushed sideways on the oar, intent on delivering his dangerous passenger as quickly as possible. Water droplets rained down upon the boatman from the casual attack, along with splinters of broken wood as the pair passed through the opening in the debris. The fisherman shuddered at the wetting, flinched as a splinter bit into a hand, but he kept back any curse he might utter.

One did not anger cultivators.

Ignorant—or deigning to ignore—the boatman, Zhao Wan searched the horizon, seeking the village and their final destination. His other hand, resting on the hilt of his jian, rubbed the spirit ring on his middle finger as he recalled the urgent summons he had received.

The Forgotten Vale Sect was a small sect as things went in the state of Shen, with four Elders in the Core Formation stage and a Patriarch who had lingered at Nascent Soul for over a half decade. Their total membership barely crossed eighty sect members, with the majority—like most immortal cultivation sects—in the Body Cleansing stage of improvement.

Even so, due to a fortuitous encounter nearly a decade ago, Cheng Zhao Wan owed one of their current Elders a favor. And if there was one thing that Zhao Wan hated with a passion, it was favors owed. It was literally inimical to his *dao* path.

Now, an opportunity to relieve himself of this karmic burden had arrived and Zhao Wan intended to take it. Even if it might require him to lower himself to digging out mortals from their sodden and wrecked villages.

Lips twisted in a grimace at that thought, Zhao Wan exhaled and tried to still his mind. It would not do to show his distaste at such a mortal endeavor. Farmers were important, fishermen as well. It was not their fault they had been born into such positions, and they certainly were better than the merchants who plied their trade and made nothing.

Still, did they all have to be so ignorant?

Unconsciously, Zhao Wan's fingers drummed against the hilt of his sword. Impatience would serve him no good, nor would speculation about the reasons for his summons. He would learn soon enough what the Forgotten Vale Sect had to ask of him.

Eventually, the village that was their destination made an appearance on the horizon. As the fisherman pushed against the single oar with renewed energy, Zhao Wan eyed the dock. It was a tattered mess, the piling on one side having broken during the recent storm, the floating portion tilting precariously with half of the dock itself still submerged. Once more, the boat owner slowed his vessel, frowning over the top of the low-slung shelter.

"Thank you for your service." Zhao Wan had noticed the problem early enough, and with their destination so close, he saw no reason to delay.

He leapt off the boat, crossing half the distance with a single movement, then touched down on the water lightly, pushing against it as he exerted his internal chi. The action was sufficient to propel him the remaining distance, and he landed lightly on a post that stuck out of the water at the shattered dock.

Behind him, the boat owner swore under his breath—though not softly enough for Zhao Wan not to hear—as the boat rocked lightly from the cultivator's swift departure. He then dipped his oar beneath the water, turning his boat around. If he paddled fast, it was possible that the exit would still be clear, and the boatman might make his way back to his village with minimal fuss. In any case, he had no desire to hang around the cultivation sect.

Bad things happened near immortals, especially to mortals.

Those who sought immortality were often embroiled in battles and other eventful tragedies, as though their very existence brought the wrath of the heavens and the twisting skeins of fate to the fore. Better for the immortals to exist in the *jianghu*[2] and the mortals in the world beside it.

Zhao Wan searched the bamboo forest before him, spotting the muddy path that led away from the lonely dock. He also noted the broken signpost, blown over, next to the head of the path. From his position, the mud-covered signpost was illegible, though he glimpsed the character for what could have been for "forget."

Choice made and without a greeting party, he leapt once more, letting his chi flow through his body and into his aura. He moved swiftly now, eager to see the end of his trip. His aura allowed him to utilize his sect's Wind Steps *qinggong*[3] method to swiftly run across the muddy ground.

---

[2] Jianghu—directly translated, rivers and lakes. Another term for the world of martial artists and immortal cultivators.

[3] Qinggong—light foot, a form of training to allow a body to move swiftly and lightly. Actual martial art technique, though obviously more awesome here.

His passing barely disturbed the earth, and even the occasional rain drop or mud splash missed him as his aura easily deflected them.

Speed was important, but a good appearance was just as necessary. After all, he was representing the Verdant Green Waters Sect here, the most powerful immortal organization in the state of Shen. Furthermore, being the youngest Elder in the sect at this time, he had the most to lose if rumors of his uncouth appearance were to spread.

***

The Forgotten Vale Sect was neither in a vale nor forgotten. Its original Patriarch—the current Patriarch's Master—had told tales of originating from such a place, hidden by mists and guarded by powerful Spirit Beasts.

His tales spoke of a land that he could never return to, for his banishment was permanent and he dared not, even when he reached the Nascent Soul Stage, challenge the leadership of his village. Of course, few believed him. Such stories were commonly created to boost the standing of an immortal cultivator who had no true lineage to call upon. Still, it was clear from the cultivation techniques and battle formations he utilized that he had acquired some lost knowledge.

Such occurrences were not uncommon.

In a land replete with powerful Spirit and Demonic Beasts, outposts of civilization could be overrun long before powerful cultivators or dutiful armies could arrive to save them. In such a world, a lucky wandering cultivator might stumble upon resources thought lost forever more.

Other tales, of cultivation caves where isolated hermits had faded away in pursuit of immortality or smaller sects slaughtered by the dark sects that plagued the jianghu, were commonly bandied about, popular stories being replete with drama and bloodshed.

In the end, no one cared so long as one could back up their wild tales with sufficient strength.

Nowadays, the Forgotten Vale Sect stood on a small rise, their pagoda-like residence overlooking the surrounding lands. What used to be rice fields sat beneath the hill, stepping down from the top to the cleared land in gradual waves. After all, even immortals had need for sustenance.

Recent flooding had seen many of these fields damaged, earthen walls broken, and gathered water flooding outward to spill below. Smaller buildings, residences for the farmers and other servants, stood mostly unharmed, dotted between these fields and steps.

Amidst all this wreckage, mortal peasants worked, their pants rolled up, their chests bare as they propped up sodden walls and sank long branches into the earth to stabilize foundations.

Others moved among the dry rice stalks in the upper fields, picking their way between the crops to destroy pests and save the harvest as best they could.

More importantly, to Zhao Wan's gaze, was the sight of the single Guardian standing aloft the sect building, uncaring about the breeze that threatened his perch. Yellow robes trimmed with purple fluttered in the wind, long dark hair streaming behind him as he watched over the surroundings. Yet as Zhao Wan neared, his gaze locked upon the cultivator.

"Welcome, fellow cultivator. to the Forgotten Vale Sect."

The voice that spoke seemed to arrive in Zhao Wan's ears without passing through the intervening space, the smallest bit of chi threading through the air the only hint of the cultivation technique in use.

"We beg forgiveness and understanding for the disarray you find our lands in."

"You have nothing to excuse. The heaven's will, and the earth sustains," Zhao Wan said, trusting the other to have a skill to pick up his words at a distance. He certainly had no such technique to project his voice, though he made a mental note to look into one in the future. "I am Elder Cheng Zhao Wan of the Verdant Green Waters Sect. My presence has been requested by Elder Tung Chee Ying."

"We have been expecting your arrival. Welcome, once more, honored guest. I am Guardian Mah. Elder Tung awaits you within on the third floor," Elder Mah replied smoothly. After offering one last nod, he turned his gaze to the surroundings once more.

Zhao Wan did not take offense, understanding that the guardian's duties required him to be on guard. In a time of calamity such as this, his duties were even more pressing. Demonic Beasts, sensing easy prey, would stalk the mortals whose regular routines and protections were in disarray.

Pouring additional chi through his body, Zhao Wan sped up further, crossing the open land. His passing raised a strong wind that fluttered robes and sent soggy leaves spraying out behind him as he ascended the hill, the peasants exclaiming in surprise at his sudden arrival. Within moments, he was at the door of the pagoda, landing lightly with the barest noise, and released the chi in his body. The pull of the earth resumed once more, making his bones and muscle ache a little at the sudden increase in weight, his hair settling just a touch faster behind him.

Sweeping his hand down his robes and feeling the precious silk slip through his fingers, Zhao Wan ensured he was presentable. Then he knocked.

The door swung open almost immediately, a boy—barely fourteen and an outer sect disciple by his drab robes—offering simple directions. Zhao Wan stepped within and turned toward the staircase alongside the outer wall. Above him, the enclosed wooden timber ceiling with its raised top allowed light to stream in, aided by spirit lights set through the building.

The pagoda itself smelled of wood, of mud and churned earth, of medicine and incense. Shuffling feet, a cough from above, the whisper of a brush on bamboo paper echoed down from above, though it was quieter than what Zhao Wan expected.

He was only required to ask directions once more when he reached the third floor, the scurrying inner sect disciple leading him directly to his benefactor's door. Yet even before he reached it, Zhao Wan's nose wrinkled. For a smell, dark and cloying like burnt tar, permeated the floor. At first in traces but growing stronger as he neared the door, such that he held a silk cloth to his nose in disgust.

His guide knocked once before stepping aside and Zhao Wan made his handkerchief disappear, knowing better than to show his distaste.

"Come." The voice was familiar, but different at the same time. Weaker and thready, unlike the deep baritone Zhao Wan recalled.

Before Zhao Wan could collect his thoughts, the door swung open, releasing a concentrated miasma of the same odor and revealing the horrific sight within.

"Oh, senior..." Zhao Wan stepped within, his voice tinged with dismay, his shock fully exposed.

Elder Tung lay on his bed, propped up on one emaciated elbow, eyes sunken and a corner of the blanket pulled down, exposing his side and revealing the creeping darkness that had infected his torso.

"Young Cheng..." Elder Tung said, gesturing Zhao Wan to his bedside. "You have grown strong and famous. The exploits of the Sundering Blade are spoken of by many."

"I could not have achieved the heights I have without senior's guidance." Zhao Wan bowed low as he crossed the distance and stopped by the bed. He schooled his face, even as the smell grew stronger now that he was near.

"A small enough thing."

"Not to me."

A tired laugh, then Elder Tung murmured, "What is a single life saved worth?"

"Everything. Nothing. It all depends on the person, does it not?" Zhao Wan replied.

Squatting with his legs folded underneath him, Zhao Wan clutched his benefactor's hand, feeling the hot and papery-thin flesh slide under his fingers. Elder Tung should have been in his mid-fifties, a healthy middle-aged cultivator; instead a scarecrow was before him, a sickened and wizened man whose hair was sparse and his eyes hollow and darkened like a panda's. Still, deep within those pain-filled eyes, a cunning light flickered.

"Modest still. Do you still follow that foolish dao you wrote to me about? What was it, a few years ago?" Chee Ying said softly. When Zhao Wan nodded, the injured man let out a laugh. "Fool still, then. No man can survive alone. Not unless they choose to be a hermit."

"Hermit perhaps, one day. But I have too many ties that must be severed first," Zhao Wan said. "I must free myself of these binding threads before I take such a step."

"But you will eventually?"

Zhao Wan could not help but nod. He would. He had to. He would ascend to the heavens free of karmic burdens, of all debts. Then he would truly be a free agent, unburdened by mortal concerns or future attachments.

"Fool, boy." Chee Ying closed his eyes. He fell so silent, his breathing so light that Zhao Wan almost thought he had fallen asleep. "So be it. I called you to relieve you of one such binding then. You may cut the thread between us, after you resolve this matter."

Zhao Wan inclined his head in thanks, even as he wondered if this act of generosity had just added to the karmic thread between them. All such thoughts were washed away as Chee Ying uttered his next words.

"I charge you, Elder Cheng Zhao Wan of the Verdant Green Waters Sect, with avenging my death. Find the dark sect members who have crept into my sect and our lands and eradicate them. One and all."

Chapter 2

Silence filled the small room. A very small room, Zhao Wan realized as he surveyed it. Strange that an Elder of a sect would have one so small. Then again, Chee Ying had always been generous to a fault.

A wooden bed adorned with a stuffed silk cushion and a wooden block to rest one's head. A raised platform to accommodate the kneeling desk and the scroll and writing implements, a small brazier and copper teapot beside it. On the other side, a bowl with the dregs of medicinal tea within. A small bottle with writing that described the pills on a simple leather tag, the calligraphy barely legible, sat beside the bowl. From the teapot, the scent of old tea rose, the contents having been forgotten and uncleaned for weeks now.

Zhao Wan frowned at that minor indication of neglect, a strange sign amidst the careful cleanliness and care of the remaining surroundings. There was not even dirt on the windowsill on the outer wall, opposite his friend's bed.

"Will you do it?" Chee Ying asked threadedly. Again.

Zhao Wan realized he had forgotten to answer his benefactor, so shocked had he been by the pronouncement. Rather than replying, he latched onto an incongruous element of that statement. "The dark sect? They were banished. Cast away decades ago. Destroyed."

"They live and thrive." Chee Ying touched his side. "This is proof enough."

Zhao Wan was no physician. He was a swordmaster, a man who had achieved the Heart of the Sword at the age of twenty-three and formed his Core at twenty-five. He was an Elder of his sect, a prodigy even among the prodigies who strutted through the kingdom of Shen. For all his skills, all his achievements, the healing of bodies was outside his skillset.

Reading the doubt in the younger man's face, Chee Ying shook his head sadly. "Go. Speak with Physician Gu. She will tell you the truth." Then his eyes drifted closed, the energy he had conjured to speak with Zhao Wan fading. "But I do not release you from your promise. Not yet. Find them. Take my revenge for me." Softer, so soft that Zhao Wan almost did not hear it, he said, "Save the orthodox sects."

Zhao Wan watched Chee Ying's eyes close, his head lolling to the side on the pillow. Zhao Wan shifted the blankets a little, making sure the older man was properly tucked away, the seeping, creeping black wound hidden. For a long moment, he stared at his benefactor, remembering the strong, powerful man who had stood in front of him, guarding his life and honor one autumn evening.

Then he strode off in search of Physician Gu and answers.

***

Logic dictated that the physician was a senior member of the sect. Custom demanded that she have an office higher up, in a place of prestige and adoration. Practicality though required her patients be seen to as quickly as possible, ensuring that her treatment rooms would be on a lower level.

Standing outside the door of Elder Cheng's room, Zhao Wan extended his spiritual sense to sweep through the building. He kept his touch light, knowing that he was a guest and should not impose his will. Even going so far as to extend his spiritual sense—his aura in a greatly diffused form—to gather the answers he desired was considered arrogant.

That was no great burden, for he was from the Verdant Green Waters Sect. As the premier sect of the kingdom, they were well-known to be arrogant cultivators. No great burden to add to that perception, and Zhao Wan was too agitated by what he'd seen to wait for a passing sect member to tell him the location of the physician, not when he had a more direct method available.

By the time his senses had reached the top and bottom of the building, Zhao Wan had located her. He descended quickly, hopping over the stair railing to fall to the bottom floor through the empty center of the pagoda. He pushed at his chi as he fell, landing with a light thump that he absorbed with the bending of his knees.

Chiding himself internally for the disturbance and his lack of practice, Zhao Wan resolved to practice his qinggong techniques further. He had a scroll for the Tempered Sky Blade in his storage ring, a flying sword technique that would have been a much more elegant method of descending. However, to make use of it, he had to achieve a greater understanding of the Wind Steps qinggong technique first.

After all, if one could not lighten one's body sufficiently, the weight imposed upon the flying sword would be too great. Flight was already onerous, and he, as a single-layer Core formation Elder, had little enough energy to spare. No. Better to train the basics first, before he took to the skies.

The least dignified thing he could think of was plummeting from the skies like a fallen bird.

Zhao Wan found the physician and her helpers in short order, following the cool energy of her aura. The crowded welcoming hall, set just off the main entrance, had been converted into a makeshift hospital, bedspreads laid across the floor and a single massive dining table set far in the depths of the hallway, formation flags sparkling around the table to hinder sight and muffle noise. A much-needed addition, for the traces of blood that ran from the table onto the wooden floor spoke of the grim business within.

Days after the flash flood, the hallway was mostly quiet, only remnants of the disaster's aftermath showcased. A discarded piece of clothing, bloody and dirty. A forgotten doll, kicked to the far corner of the building. Piles of dirty laundry waiting to be washed, stuffed in a corner. Muddy tracks being scrubbed away by outer sect cultivators on their hands and knees. And, of course, the patients, lying asleep or propped up, whispering to one another, with their broken and bandaged bodies.

Making his way to the end of the hallway, Zhao Wan judged the mortals who rested there with practiced ease. Not even one had opened more than a few base meridians, even though the Yellow Emperor's cultivation manual had been taught to them all by imperial decree.

Lazy, foolish, or just untalented, each and every one of them.

"You." The voice brought Zhao Wan's attention to the forefront, as the physician stepped through the curtain of energy surrounding the table. Her eyes darted to his sword, then to his clothing. "You're the sword prodigy, are you not?"

"Some have—"

"Good. Come with me." Bemused, Zhao Wan closed the remaining distance, only to back away as she thrust a single-edged, highly sharpened thin blade at him. Hilt first, at least. "Take this. I need you to do the cut."

"Me?" Zhao Wan made no move to take the knife, going so far as to cross his arms.

"Yes, you. Place your sword intent into this blade and cut off his leg." Physician Gu gestured inward at the one she spoke of, a patient tied to the table and half delirious with a fever and a mangled left foot, blood dribbling from the torniqueted wound. "I'll point out where to chop. The man's a Body Cultivator, and he reinforced his bones first, the fool." She shook her head in exasperation. "Now, hurry. He is bleeding out."

"I will not," Zhao Wan said. "His fate is his. I will not add his suffering or his salvation to my own karmic balance."

"You…!" Physician Gu's voice rose a little before she jerked her chin, discarding his objection. She darted back, her voice rising as she spoke to her attendants. "Hand me the saw. And hold him still!"

Zhao Wan felt a flicker of empathy run through him as he stepped back, exiting the formation. He felt the energy of the formation part around his aura, the sense of what occurred behind the formation fading a little.

He understood the Physician's needs, but he would not bend. His dao, his path to immortality, required him to free himself from karmic threads. Saving the life of another, one whom he had no familiarity with or prior obligation to, was anathema to his way.

Cries of pain and the grinding of saw on toughened bone rose from the table, and the formation flickered as it strained under the screaming voice. Zhao Wan turned away, knowing there was little here for him at the moment. As he did so, he spotted a little boy crouched just outside the formation flags, clutching a stuffed pig made of dried grass and remnant hemp, large brown eyes wide with fear.

A hand raised then dropped, Zhao Wan pushing aside his own weakness as he strode through the doors he had entered. It was not his place to change the boy's fate. He would not bend.

Instead, he exited the building to find the training grounds set behind the pagoda. If he was to wait, then he would train.

The training ground for the Forgotten Vale Sect was in disarray, the sect having more important work to undertake than cleaning the empty courtyard of cut stone and pressed earth.

Mud, leaves, and broken branches littered the stone flooring, wooden training pinions coated in mud and lying on their sides. Weapons racks lay scattered across the grounds, their contents missing.

Eyeing the floor with distaste, Zhao Wan let his gaze turn toward the plum flower piles outside the stone courtyard. The three dozen poles, each a foot and a half in diameter, were sunk into the earth to varying heights. The tallest stood over ten feet tall, the shortest a bare foot above the ground. The drunken staircase-like arrangement of the plum flower piles was formed in bunches of "flowers," each flower made of a central stamen and four petal poles.

The piles were dirty, washed-up branches, leaves, and even a discarded training dao beneath them. Dirty they might be and their footing treacherous, but as his old master would note, that meant it was good practice.

Flooding his aura with chi once more, Zhao Wan leapt lightly onto the first post. His front foot brushed another raised pole lightly as he took his stance, a hand on the hilt of his sword. Breathing deeply, he settled his mind, casting the intrusive reminders of his humanity and the cries of a crippled mortal from his mind.

Inhale.

Exhale.

Move.

Zhao Wan drew and stepped, the first motion a sword draw. He chose the eighth form of the Sundering Blade to practice. It was new, it was unrefined, it was difficult. All the better.

The greater the challenge, the greater the degree of concentration he required.

The plum blossom piles with their varying heights and their slippery footing were just another obstacle to perfection.

Parting the Thread, stepping upward with a cross-body draw to settle on the next pile. Take the sword sheath from the belt at the same time, for the Scholar's Rebuke could transition to Passing the Letter with the other arm. The sword thrust could be executed as a stable-bodied lunge or a passing step, all to allow him to cross over the center pile and ascend ever higher.

Each motion was executed slowly. Excruciatingly so. Even when he transitioned over the piles in his lunge, he maintained his balance and rate of motion, chi-enhanced muscles locked into place. Movements as sure as a paint brush, focused and fluid. As he ascended, Zhao Wan tested the motions in his mind, battling imaginary enemies and varying options on reflex as he danced his own unique form.

Passing the Wet Brush with his sheathed blade was too overt, easy to read as he transitioned from the earlier Fanning the Flames. Useful perhaps as a feint, but only against the most pedestrian of opponents who could not read intent and trickery without the aid of a courtesan.

No, a more subtle transition was required.

Offering of the wooden Cane, allowing the sheath to spin and strike at his opponent's arm, extended his range and made the attack vectors more varied—allowing blows from the side and top—as well as setting up the next movement. A kick, rather than a blade strike, changing levels now as he dropped low. A roundhouse to the lead leg or a sweep to both, either could work.

Zhao Wan crossed the plum blossom piles in exquisitely graceful, slow motion, his mind subsumed within the dance of blades and imaginary opponents. As for the screaming mortal, the doe-eyed child, and the angry and disappointed physician…

Those could come later.

For now, there was only Zhao Wan and his jian.

His path as the Sundering Blade.

And nothing else.

As it should be.

Chapter 3

Physician Gu found him hours later, still practicing. Her arms were crossed, her face pinched when she exited the building and crossed to the training grounds. Upon sensing her presence, Zhao Wan leapt off the plum blossom piles to greet her, sheathing his sword as he flew gracefully through the air.

"Physician Gu. It is an honor to speak with you," Zhao Wan said.

"I cannot say the same."

"My dao path does not allow me to—"

"I do not care." Physician Gu raised her chin, staring down her nose at Zhao Wan. Her distaste was clear, in both gaze and tone of voice. "If you were not Elder Tung's guest, I would have moved to have you removed from our lands already."

"Then I am grateful for your forbearance."

"You had questions. Ask."

"Elder Tung's wounds. Tell me about them."

A flicker of regret and further anger, before her face smoothed out to dispassionate impartiality. "The wounds are fatal. Necrotic energy has infiltrated, spreading through his body and destroying his meridians. Eventually they will reach his dantian and he will die. He battles it even now, but it will consume him at some point. All I have been able to do is slow down the process."

"How did his injury happen?"

Physician Gu shook her head. "I know not. He arrived back in our sect a month and a half ago, sporting the wound. I bandaged it as requested, applied the usual herbs and compresses. It grew worst almost immediately.

"There is, I fear, nothing more I can do." She frowned. "I know not even what caused it nor the why of it." That hurt her professional pride it seemed, for her voice grew less dispassionate as she spoke. "I noted a deep wound on his torso when he arrived, but the damage was too significant to tell what had caused it. Elder Tung was not able to provide further clarification."

"Why?" Zhao Wan said. "Surely he must know something."

"He claims to have been caught for days in an illusion formation at the time, where he was assailed by both friends and foe alike. Rather than lay boundless claims of who his attacker was, Elder Tung chose to say nothing."

"Leaving me with no leads," Zhao Wan said, frustrated. He wondered if he could make his benefactor speak to him, but false leads could be as dangerous to the investigation as real hints.

"No. Though…"

He made an inquiring noise deep in his throat.

The physician cast a glance upward, toward the top of the pagoda before she waved a hand just beneath her nose. "The wound, and the damage it causes, has a particular scent."

"Scent?" Zhao Wan said, surprised. "Do you mean the rot?"

"No. Something more, something unique to it."

Zhao Wan frowned.

"You would not notice it. It requires a sense technique. Our founder brought one with him that is part of our foundation, though it is practiced mostly by those of us who serve."

Zhao Wan nodded, having heard of such techniques before. Sense techniques, beyond sight and hearing, were uncommon but not unusual.

"It requires practice for one to grasp it as an extension on the base expansion of our senses. For a physician, a sensitive sense of smell is highly useful." She touched her nose with a small self-satisfied smile. "The changes in a body can often be noticed through the alteration of a body's chi flows and humors long before it is visible." Then, almost as an afterthought, "Also, few cultivators actually bother to hide their cultivation level from the sense of smell."

Zhao Wan looked down, surreptitiously sniffing at himself. He had to admit, he had never considered altering or suppressing his natural scent. He did not smell—constant and regular baths ensured that—and beyond that, controlling one's aura was always the first step. Even the most oblivious Core Formation cultivator would gain a basic sense of auras by the time they ascended, and most gained not just an expansion on their spiritual sense but a visual cultivation exercise at the lower, Energy Storage stage.

Still, the idea that he was, for all intents and purposes, entirely unprotected from discernment—even if it was only via one sense—was an uncomfortable one.

"These exercises, are they hard?" Zhao Wan asked. He would not ask for the exercise itself, not with the hint that it was a sect secret.

Certainly not from her. For one thing, she would not have the right to provide it. For another, he wanted to avoid such entanglements. Still, the Verdant Green Waters would have a similar exercise if it was not a rare one.

"Not at all. I started training as a Body Cleansing cultivator."

"Ah. Thank you for that information," Zhao Wan said, offering a small bow.

If even a Body Cleansing cultivator could learn this, perhaps he could muddy his way through a cultivation exercise of his own. Mildly dangerous, but not too much. A Core Formation cultivator could more easily absorb the backlash from the small trickle of chi while experimenting than a Body Cleansing cultivator.

"Is there anything further you wish to know?"

"Yes. He claimed this was the work of the dark sect. Why would he do so?"

"The wound itself, I assume," Physician Gu said. "It is, as mentioned, nothing like anything I have seen before. The damage, the way it spreads, all of it."

"Not a Demonic Beast taking an unknown dao path in its evolution?" he offered.

"That would be my assumption. His beliefs, his memories of what happened—or did not happen—could all be a delusion caused by the wound."

Zhao Wan nodded and fell silent. So silent and for so long that she eventually turned to leave, only to be stopped by his voice.

"Is there any recommendation you might have if I were to encounter the source of the wound? Anything to stop its progress?"

Physician Gu took on a contemplative look, dark brown eyes turning inward. She eventually shrugged. "Do not let it touch you. But if it does, I recommend severing the limb as quickly as possible. It is the only way to be certain." Smiling grimly, she bowed. "If that is all?"

"It is."

Zhao Wan watched her leave, a little frown on his face as she disappeared into the building. Then, sensing attention turned on him that pressed upon his aura, he looked upward. A single figure, high above, stared down at him. When that figure noticed Zhao Wan's gaze, he beckoned him up.

Letting out a long slow breath, the cultivator sighed. It seemed it was finally time to meet the Patriarch of the Forgotten Vale Sect. And do his best to avoid further entanglements.

***

The room the Patriarch of the Forgotten Vale Sect met him in was just below the top of the pagoda, what with the topmost room being home to the protective array that covered the sect and allowed the Protector to view their lands in detail.

Even if it was not the most prominent position in the building, the Patriarch's abode was luxurious, with mother-of-pearl rosewood furniture, silk coverings, and feather-stuffed cushions being among the least of the furnishings within. Lounging against a chair by a tea table with cups of newly poured tea, the Patriarch waited.

"Cheng Zhao Wan of the Verdant Green Waters greets the Patriarch of the Forgotten Vale," Zhao Wan intoned the moment he caught sight of the man, bowing low and offering him a clasped hand greeting. He kept himself bowed until the Patriarch had returned the greeting and waved him up.

"Elder Cheng, it is a pleasure to have one of such great fame come to visit our minor sect," the Patriarch said.

"Patriarch Zhen, you do me too much of an honor," Zhao Wan said. "I am here because of the debt I owe Elder Tung. It is I who is honored to be here."

"Ah, the debt and his summons." Patriarch Zhen shook his head, his long, wispy beard moving from side to side. He gestured for Zhao Wan to accompany him and take a seat, the small tea table between the pair as they sat. A small tea set was on the table, a metal pot set over a brazier heating water and releasing a tiny trickle of steam by the side. "He has spoken to me, in confidence and publicly, of his beliefs."

"And your thoughts on the matter, Patriarch?" Zhao Wan asked.

"Much like my physician, I believe that Elder Tung's views of what might have happened or will happen to be misguided. Whatever it is that effects Little [4] Tung, it is unlikely to be the actions of a group that have long been destroyed."

"And yet, the dark sects do live on. In other kingdoms, in other sects. Could they not be extending their tendrils here?" Zhao Wan offered. He did not believe what he said, not truly, but to see his benefactor's beliefs so easily discarded hurt something in him. Perhaps because such a reflection of opinion was a mark against him too.

"Perhaps. But why target us then? Here?" The Patriarch gestured around him. "We are neither on the border nor prominent. We are a minor sect, in a minor location of little

---

[4] I'm using Little as a literal translation. Often, terms like "big" or "small / little" are an indicator of affection when added to the name in replacement of another designation. It's also an indicator of rank and standing at the same time. As such, Little Tung indicates an affectionate relationship between the Patriarch and Elder Tung.

importance. Even if they chose to act against us, defying all logic, why target Elder Tung? Why let him escape?"

Zhao Wan had no answer. It did seem improbable that any poison or other man-made action would be done so sloppily as to allow their victim to escape—unless the man had stumbled upon the entire incident by accident. Even then, coincidence stretched belief.

Much more likely a Demonic Beast or some other unknown spirit creature was the cause of this. There were still many strange beasts and flora they had yet to catalogue.

"Then, it seems, if the belief is that the wound was dealt by a creature of some form, it falls onto me to deal with it," Zhao Wan said. "If I kill it and bring back its spirit stone, perhaps it will offer the physician enough clues of how to help the Elder."

"We can only hope." Patriarch Zhen smiled grimly. "Ask of anything we might offer you.

Little as it may be, for our resources are stretched thin."

"Because of the flood."

"Yes."

Curious that. Bad timing? Or something else? Zhao Wan disliked the idea of coincidence but having studied the flow of karma and fate for so long, he knew better than to entirely discount random coincidence in the shapings of man and destiny.

Unfortunately, the reverse could be true. The gods were fickle, and karma wove a complicated web. What might seem like coincidence at first could reveal an immortal guiding hand later.

After brief consideration, Zhao Wan said, "There is one thing. The physician mentioned a technique for amplifying the sense of smell. I understand it is a sect technique, but she spoke of it as though it was important. Your thoughts on the matter?"

"Hah. My Master's technique is of minor importance." Patriarch Zhen chuckled. "It is no private technique. We teach it to even our outer sect members who would accept it."

"Then, if you would. It seems it might be useful in the search for the culprit."

"Good, good. My Master will smile upon us today then, for converting another to his favorite technique." Patriarch Zhen chuckled to himself, an amused light dancing in his eyes. He tapped the table with two fingers. As he raised his hand, a scroll was left behind. "The Hundred Delights and A Thousand Miseries sensing technique, as requested."

Zhao Wan's eyebrow twitched. What kind of name was that?

"A truthful one."

Zhao Wan forced himself not to react. The Patriarch was not reading his mind, just anticipating his reaction. Perhaps even catching micro-changes in expression that he was unable to suppress. That was, after all, what made Nascent Soul cultivators so dangerous.

Well, among other things.

Another thought struck Zhao Wan. Did his smell change and give away his thoughts? Was he that open a book? And if so, how did he stop it? It was a vulnerability that he disliked knowing he had, even if it was not directly fatal. Still, as a Core Formation elder of the Verdant Green Waters, he understood more than most the danger of a misplaced word or emotion.

"Thank you, Honored Patriarch. I shall ensure this payment is appropriately covered," Zhao Wan said.

Already, he sensed the thread, minor as it was, curling out from the Patriarch and through him to the rest of the sect for the document. Another binding created. He wondered at his choice to take it. But it was no more onerous than the one he had formed when he had decided to hunt down the perpetrators of Elder

Tung's wound. Much would be wiped away when that was done.

In the end, all threads would be banished by the successful completion of the task he had set for himself. And if not, he would find some technique to pay them back. A minor thing from the Sect or perhaps a sword formation.

Simple. Or so he believed, at least.

Karma and fate were no simple matters to weigh, even for an expert.

Chapter 4

Zhao Wan had hoped to take his leave of the sect as quickly as he had arrived, for he saw no reason to further complicate this trip. Hunting down a Demonic Beast, or the source of the wound in Elder Tung's side, could take weeks or even months.

At least the Patriarch had been able to provide him with a location to start from, for Elder Tung had been looking into a set of ruins newly uncovered before he had stumbled back, injured and tired. Unfortunately, between the flash flood and the length of Elder Tung's expedition, he could have wandered over a hundred li from that location, all of which Zhao Wan might have to search.

More concerning was the damage the flood might have done to any traces of Elder Tung's passing. Not just physical markings—most of which would have washed away through the normal passage of time—but also the recollections of the mortals who might live nearby. Many villages had been destroyed and mortals killed by the calamity.

The wanderings of a cultivator—powerful or not—might hold little interest to them. Though Zhao Wan could hope that was not the case.

With these thoughts of a long expedition, Zhao Wan stopped in the kitchen to acquire provisions for the weeks ahead. There would be little enough available in the villages, and even here, the mortal who ran the kitchen was less than enthusiastic at parting with the sacks of rice and dried meat requested of him.

Thankfully, the Patriarch's largesse and command still held sway, though it took Zhao Wan a good quarter hour before he finally managed to pry himself free of the social niceties. Stepping on the pathway leading farther west, he found himself confronted by the final Elder of the sect.

"You are the Sundering Blade, are you not?" The man who spoke was uncommonly tall, standing a good foot above Zhao Wan. Clad in the yellow and purple of the Elders in the sect, the man sported a neatly trimmed mustache and bushy eyebrows that failed to hide the gleam of interest in his eyes. Lines etched across his face, the mustache a little white. He was slightly on the portly side too, all signs of his greater age.

"Some call me that," Zhao Wan said.

"Good. Fight me!" Hand falling to his sheathed sword breakers on his hip, the Elder slid a foot backward.

"I will not," Zhao Wan said. "It would be discourteous to battle you, as a guest of your sect."

"Bah! You are leaving anyway. And I am asking for this battle. A friendly exchange of pointers." Eagerly and bombastically the man spoke, even as he drew the sword breakers from his hips.

The weapons were similar to swords in overall design, though they were rectangular with blunted edges and much thicker than any normal blade. The weapon was meant to use its weight and density to beat other weapons aside, or bend and break the opponent's sword.

As he was about to decline once again, Zhao Wan felt a stirring deep within his soul. His lips compressed, and he sent his spiritual senses within where his chi surged through him almost without summoning.

Chi reached his eyes, touching upon his aura and his pupils, and spread further, joining him to the skeins of fate as the Eyes of Heaven Turning flared into activity. He saw the threads that spread from his chest to the world outside, connecting him to this dirty, callous world and all those who held him down.

Elder Tung, the Patriarchs of the Verdant Green Waters and the Forgotten Vale, his relatives who felt they were still owed some small regard.

Even the man before him.

It was faint, unlike the thread between him and Elder Tung. Not something that had been formed in this life, but one created as Zhao Wan walked the wheel of life over and over. Faint, easy to cut if he so chose, but even easier to...

"Yes."

"You don't have to—" The man froze as he parsed Zhao Wan's answer. "You will? You will!"

"But not here. In a proper place."

Turning on his heel, Zhao Wan treaded toward the back of the building, loosening his muscles as he moved. Forcing himself to relax with each step, letting his spiritual sense touch upon the thread that stretched between them.

It was not a real thread, not something one could put their hands upon or tie into a scarf. Yet it was genuine too, as real as the obligations a child had to a parent, a peasant to his lord, or a king to the will of heaven. One could choose to ignore such threads, but fate and heaven would bind you nevertheless, ensure the payment of these obligations in this life or the next.

Years spent meditating, casting bones and sticks, reading tea leaves and the flight of birds had honed Zhao Wan's understanding of the flow of fate and the skeins of karma. He was no expert—how could a mortal be an expert in such a subject?—but he had learned to read the knots between this life and the past. Sense unpaid obligations and previous sins come home to roost.

He could not name the exact incident, for Grandmother Meng's soup had taken such knowledge. Yet he could sense the shape of it, gain the impression of the battle and the beating. Zhao Wan understood enough. Not just what he had to do now, but what was required to dissolve this thread.

Funny, how lives once touched in the past came together in the present.

It could almost make a man laugh.

"Here." Zhao Wan turned, standing in the middle of the still wrecked training yard. The floor was uneven, branches and mud making the footing treacherous. Formations meant to keep those within and without safe had been destroyed. "Forms only."

The other Elder made a face but, glancing around the training yard, offered a reluctant nod. Rash though he might be, the man understood the necessity of containing their enthusiasm. Without the proper formations, their battle could destroy the remainder of the training field and damage the sect building itself.

Both sword breakers were drawn, touching together as he brought them to his forehead before swinging them down in salute. "Shan Lin, Elder of the Forgotten Vale Sect. Ploughing Oxen Style."

"Cheng Zhao Wan. Elder of the Verdant Green Waters Sect. The Sundering Blade." He drew his jian as he spoke, returning the salute before falling into a high guard. Hilt held high, tip pointed at his opponent's forehead. The tactical choice was unconscious, intuitive. Do not offer the blade to be struck, for his opponent would destroy it if given the chance.

The first to move was Shan Lin, the Elder sliding his feet forward in long, sweeping motions. He never allowed his foot to leave the ground, choosing to sweep aside debris rather than chance his footing. Zhao Wan, on the other hand, circled left, his steps light as a feather. Even when he came into contact with the occasional stray branch, his balance was not thrown off, his weight reduced by the Wind Step method of his sect such that he never disturbed the earth he stood upon.

Shan Lin continued to narrow the distance, the rustle of leaves and the squish of mud preceding each motion. Zhao Wan's movements were silent but for the slight noise of his breathing and the flutter of his silk robes in the wind. The scents of overturned mud, waterlogged earth, and rotting leaves filled the air, with the hint of sword oil and iron mixed within.

Six feet away, within the Sundering Blade's full lunge, Shan Lin chose to act. Leading the fight once again, he exploded from his stance, a wave of dirt and mud pushed ahead of his feet as he charged. Stone cracked with a sharp retort, even as sword breakers hummed with chi as they were brought down, one after the other in sweeping motions meant to beat aside a weapon.

Zhao Wan weaved from side to side, dodging the attacks even as he threatened his opponent with his own sword tip. Small disengages, retractions, and shifting angles kept his weapon free of encumbrance. Chi and sword intent mixed, allowing energy to surround his weapon and extend its range such that the ghostly blade of force intent threatened his opponent.

Probing energy was battered aside, each extension shattered by the bright yellow and brown energy pulsing from the sword breaker. Fast as Zhao Wan was, the paired weapons were heavy and meant to crush and shatter, trailing chi strikes leaving behind wide trails of energy. Entirely unlike the delicate weavings of the jian that darted around like a sparrow, searching for an opening.

From the second form of the Sundering Blade, Zhao Wan wove his attacks. The Scholar's Refusal drew his jian backward along his ribs, barely dodging an overhead chop. The Second Call, a wrist strike that targeted the fingers of his opponent's hand, was blocked, the tip skittering along the edge of the guarding hilt as his opponent raised his own wrist. The Hero's Fall had Zhao Wan dodge the return strike from Shan Lin, even as he pointed his tip toward the ground, intent on a sweep.

All across the training ground, the pair flowed. Form met form, Zhao Wan intent on avoiding the blades and striking at his opponent. Like the rampaging oxen of his style's name, Shan Lin ploughed straight ahead, his sword breakers connected to one another like the horns of an ox. Much like Shan Lin's namesake, any glancing blow that Zhao Wan managed to score bounced off the dull brown glow of a protective aura shell, leaving the man unharmed.

Refusal to meet his opponent or not, more skilled fighter or not, Zhao Wan couldn't avoid every attack. Shan Lin was no mewling babe with the blade but a martial expert like him. In time, feints were read, his style discerned.

The aura coating of Zhao Wan's blade took a beating as he was forced to turn aside strikes meant for head and body, the momentous swings cracking the protective shell of his own chi. The very concept of these weapons fought against Zhao Wan's control as he was forced back, step by step.

Deep within, the cultivator felt the string twist and fray, each blow that he received transmitted deeper. An old debt was being extracted, injuries and harm accumulated wearing away at the ancient debt. Understanding and enlightenment glimmered as Zhao Wan accepted the attacks further, allowing himself to be pushed back as he paid the price for a past life's impetuousness.

Then, to his surprise, Shan Lin jumped back. On reflex, Zhao Wan moved to pursue before he caught himself, bringing his movements to a stop. He held his blade in a mid-guard, frowning as Shan Lin dropped his weapons to the side, face twisted in frustration.

"What are you doing?" he cried.

"Trading pointers. Did we not agree to that?" Zhao Wan said.

"You are not even trying!" Shan Lin growled, obviously incensed. "The Sundering Blade is a prodigy of the martial realm. A man who achieved the Heart of the Blade before turning twenty-five. What I see before me is a cowering fool, refusing to do more than chip away at me.

"Where is the speed and aggressiveness that is spoken of across the thirteen counties? Where is the cutting edge feared by the sword prodigies of the Night Whispering Blade? Am I so poor an opponent that you will not show me even one of the final forms?"

Each word was like a knife into Zhao Wan's heart. Each incensed statement regrew the thread that had begun to fray, as present and past insults piled upon one another.

This was why Zhao Wan hated interacting with others. Karma was not so simply resolved, fate not so easily turned aside. There was a debt between him and Shan Lin, and it had to be settled.

Or severed.

"You do not want to face my blade in truth," Zhao Wan said, for he feared that option. It was his final recourse, but there were consequences to its use.

"I do."

"You may be injured."

"I do not care. A man must be bold to grow."

"Fool."

A grin was Shan Lin's only answer.

Zhao Wan let out a breath, sheathing his blade. He turned his body a little, letting his weight drop down even as he kept his hand on the hilt. When he next spoke, he did so coldly. "Remember. You asked for this."

Shan Lin could not help but grin, his eyes wide with delight. He raised his weapons, ready to strike, ready to receive Zhao Wan's attack.

"The first form of the Sundering Blade. The Karma Severing Cut."

Then, Zhao Wan struck.

Chapter 5

Zhao Wan left the sect with a pounding headache and a throbbing body. Heavenly chi had assaulted him once more, scouring his meridians and attacking his cultivation base for the affront of his technique. He had managed to keep the damage to the minimum; but even so, he felt as though he had spent the past two days exercising nonstop, carrying rice bags up the mountain.

Behind him, Shan Lin lay on the ground, a deep cut across his chest and a blissful—if pained—smile on his face. His eyes were blank as he took in whatever enlightenment Zhao Wan's actions had left him with. Those happy eyes were staring upward at the sky itself that had parted, clouds shifting to escape the pressure of the single cut even as beneath Shan Lin's back and feet, the earth had been ploughed in a straight line from the Sundering Blade.

For all the damage done on the world outside, it was within that Zhao Wan felt the effects the most. The thread binding him and Shan Lin had been cut, their fated connection severed. The rebound effect, as the one who had forcibly parted their fates, still poured through his chest and soul, the core that sheltered the Nascent Immortal Soul within him strained.

It would take weeks for the damage to heal. Until then, using the technique again would be dangerous. It was a fool's move to use it on a man who had so little connection—and yet, it had been necessary. If Zhao Wan was to learn, to grow in his technique and withstand greater and greater severings, he must start small. Just as a student must learn the basic brush strokes before he could compose a poem, he too had to study the effects of minor severings.

Till one day, he cut himself free of this earth and all its filthy, uncouth practices.

Steps, mortal steps, took him down the hill. He dared not churn his chi to lighten himself, so he took the mortal road now. It would take a little for his soul to settle, for the pain to subside. Even his breathing was out of place, constrained and tight.

Frowning, Zhao Wan breathed out hard while holding a hand up to his nose. He stared at the trickle of blood and the bloody glob that splattered his hand, then turned to the side and cleared his nose properly, holding a handkerchief to it. Anger flared as he compressed his nose, waiting for the bleeding to end.

Foolish, stupid, idiotic decisions in past lives. How could he have tied himself to a soul that burnt with such brutish nature? How could he have let himself be tied down then? What fool thought had made him accept the man's challenge?

Of course he would have to cut himself free.

No one, not even a boorish idiot like Shan Lin, could have believed Zhao Wan was likely to lose. Him, lose? To someone as ungraceful as Shan Lin?

Foolishness.

No, this was better. Even if it hurt all the way down to his toes and the trip to where Elder Tung had been injured might take longer. In the meantime, he could review his form, what mistakes he had made when he had separated himself and Elder Shan.

He would use this event to work out how better to handle the backlash, how to carve out such an exception from himself and the one he severed without drawing the ire of heaven.

As Zhao Wan strode down the muddy roadway, replete with branches and ruts from passing wagons, his gaze was drawn to a bush by the side. A tunic lay draped over it, as though cast aside by a forgetful peasant and not left behind by receding flood water.

He knew there was a way to cut himself free with minimal punishment. After all, he was not the only one who saw fit to bend fate and karma to his will.

Floods, typhoons, cyclones, and lightning strikes. Calamity, rained down from above. Peaches of immortality served on a plate to generous peasants, and purses of gold left beneath boulders blocking the way.

Twists of fate and karma, delivered from up high.

The heavens bent the world to their whims without care or consideration. They danced upon dreams and fed nightmares in equal measure. All to follow their own daos.

So why not do the same as a mortal?

If it was arrogant to think that, overwhelming pride was the hallmark of all cultivators. Each and every one of them chose to stand against the turning of fate itself, to challenge old age, death, and the repeating cycle of rebirth.

Cultivation was an affront to the heavens and immortality the ultimate prize.

***

That evening, Zhao Wan found himself under the boughs of a tree, his sword propped against his shoulder, a merry fire crackling before him as a small pot of rice simmered over it. There was no roadside inn to stay within this night, the buildings meant for travelers collapsed as slick ground had given way beneath it. No, tonight, Zhao Wan would sleep under the stars.

Like a damn peasant.

The indignities a man must suffer. Turning his mind away from his uncomfortable future, Zhao Wan leaned over to check on his porridge. The shiitake mushrooms he had set within bubbled happily, slices of wild ginger and onions having joined the shredded portions of salted fish to give the meal flavor. One of the simplistic meals that he had learned to cook for himself to stave off hunger.

Nothing like the feasts back home, but he had neither the time nor patience to learn such techniques when he had better things to do. Like practice his forms.

"Doesn't smell that bad."

The voice that interrupted his internal grumbling had Zhao Wan reaching for his sword, eyes narrowed. The fact that Shan Lin did not seem perturbed by the greeting he received, going so far as to find a stump to drag over to sit on next to him, had Zhao Wan even more surprised. Almost as much as the man's ability to sneak up on him.

"I'll share what I brought, if you'll share what you cooked."

"What are you doing here?" Zhao Wan said warily.

"Eating. I hope."

"I meant, here. With me."

"Joining you. I thought that was obvious."

"I did not ask for help."

"That's okay. My father never knew how to ask for help either. We learnt to work around him. I'm good at that," Shan Lin replied. "Fixing houses is not a thing for a single person, no matter how strong you are."

"Your father was a carpenter?" Zhao Wan found himself asking, distracted by the random piece of information offered.

"He was. A good one too. We worked in the cities mostly, generally around here. It was a good living for a long time, kept the family fed." The big man grinned. "Me in school. And when the sects knew I had some talent, they took me in."

Zhao Wan found himself shaking his head, having no desire to learn more of the man's life story. He regretted asking, for he feared the reformation of the thread. "Again, why are you here?"

"The Patriarch thinks at least one of us should come with you." The big man finished clearing a spot on the ground and laid a small table on it, the table drawn from his storage ring.

Zhao Wan had to suppress a flash of jealousy, for it was obvious the Elder had a bigger compressed spatial space in his ring than him. Rings with a decent amount of space were hard to acquire. Finding an individual with the right dao of space and the training and inclination to build one could be difficult, especially as most storage rings broke down over time.

"He wanted to send some junior, but after that beating, I knew I had to follow," Shan Lin said.

"Why?"

"I have a lot more to learn, of course!"

"I am not teaching you. Nor agreeing to have you here."

"That's okay. I know about you, Sundering Blade."

"And what do you know?" Zhao Wan asked, eyes narrowing a little.

"Everyone knows of the newest prodigy of the Verdant Green Waters, his antisocial behavior, and his karmic dao." Shan Lin gestured with his hand, eyes sparkling as he continued. "It's the main gossip among the Elders of the kingdom. And the biggest betting pool."

"Betting pool?"

"Oh yes. Some think you'll be changing your dao soon. Others that you'll ascend in the next twenty years. Lots of different bets. Most around at what point you'll stall out." Shan Lin ticked each of these options off on his fingers. "Then there're the bets on the number of duels you'll be conducting. Honor duels. Those to break or destroy your karmic debt. The amount of time you'll take to visit another sect." Humor now glinting in his eyes, Shan Lin added, "I won a lot of taels on that last one."

Arms crossing in annoyance, Zhao Wan growled. "I did not know I was the talk of so many."

"Eh, that's what old people do." Shan Lin stroked his mustache, patting down the sides. "At a certain point, your growth slows. And then there's not much else to do, beyond cultivating and taking care of the sect and the children beneath us. That takes time, but it isn't interesting. Talking about newcomers, studying them, can be useful. It's why so many of us end up with students. At the least, it's interesting."

Zhao Wan snorted. The idea of taking a student of any kind was anathema to him. Tying himself to another for so long would be against the very principles of his dao. He could not imagine a circumstance beyond the most dire one to make such a choice.

"In any case, your presence is unwanted," Zhao Wan said. "Leave."

"No."

"I said, you are not needed."

"That's fine. But my Patriarch has commanded me to be here. And I intend to." Shan Lin leaned forward. "And you can't stop me. Unless you intend to kill me. And incur another binding."

"That's not the only way to stop you," Zhao Wan said threateningly. It was a hollow threat. He dared not use his blade on the other. Nor would it be as effective. Without a thread to sever, the damage he could do the other was limited.

A fatal flaw in his technique that he cared not to explain. Or reveal.

"Then go ahead. But I'm not leaving." Shan Lin bent down, picking up the bun he had laid on the table. A small display of food was before them now, the man having taken a sumptuous meal from his ring. To Zhao Wan's surprise, most of it still steamed too. An unusual occurrence after being deposited in a storage ring, which often leached heat from their contents. "Bun?"

Ignoring the offered meal, Zhao Wan continued to glare at the other. In the end, he turned away. The man was right. Zhao Wan could not afford to fight him, not without incurring the wrath of the Patriarch or influencing his own fate. Considering the goal of this entire event was to reduce his karmic burden, the best he could do was ignore Shan Lin and hope that his obstinance would only create the most minor of threads. Eventually, Zhao Wan would cut them again, but small threads of mutual companionship were unimportant.

Or so he theorized at least.

Once again, Zhao Wan found himself wondering about his own path.

In the end, it was what it was. He had chosen a path and he would not shy away from it, no matter how wrong it might be. When it came to dao paths, there was as great a danger in being indecisive as being mistaken. Perhaps more.

So resolved, Zhao Wan spooned the porridge into his bowl and ignored the loud, messy, and tantalizing meal eaten just before him. Content to walk his own path, for now.

Chapter 6

The next day, Cheng Zhao Wan rose early. Not because he was being hounded by a persistent, obnoxious cultivator but because that was his routine. He woke early, he slept late, and he cultivated when he could. He was, in essence, a disciplined man. He did not vary his routine much.

What was not part of his routine was his immediate departure, leaving his hopeful companion behind in his luxurious tent, without even spending a moment to boil himself a cup of tea or practice his blade. Instead, Zhao Wan took off down the pathway, moving with alacrity.

The muddy roadway, portions of its reinforced structure washed away by the floods, was slowly drying. The ground was no longer filled with muddy puddles and strewn leaves but had dried to a deceptive hardness that was slick under the cloth shoes the cultivator wore. Luckily, a minor and constant use of his qinggong methods kept him as light as the wind, allowing him to skim across the ground without marring the drying landscape and leaving little trace of his passing.

He moved fast all day, leaving struggling mortals and destroyed farmland behind in equal measure. It was only toward the end of the day that the gaps between outposts of civilization expanded further, the concentric circles of villages and their fields being farther and farther pushed apart by strips of untamed wilderness.

Zhao Wan crossed tens of li that day, moving at a good clip, even as his damaged soul throbbed at the exercise. Burdened only with the smallest of bags, hand resting on the pommel of his sword, he loped onward with unceasing energy.

His presence was noticed and remarked upon by the peasants he passed. Many ducked their heads low. A few even went so far as to prostate themselves on the ground. It was a good sign that it was only a few, an indication of the overall benevolence of the Forgotten Vale Sect.

Few mortals could be expected to stand up to or dare to offer even the mildest rebuke to a true cultivator. Though most had received some form of training in the cultivation arts, the difference in strength between a true cultivator and them was as great as heaven and earth. It was no wonder that your average mortal sought to appease these mini-demi-gods as they blew through their lives.

It was also why the rules of the jianghu were so enshrined in custom.

Mortals and cultivators lived separate, if adjacent lives. Interacting only at the apex of events and bureaucracy, serving the emperor and the kingdom but left alone otherwise. It was a protection, in customs and form, for both sides.

Immortal cultivators, in their search and longer lifespans, removed themselves from the daily interactions of mere mortals to save themselves heartache and focus upon their own progress. Mortals, allowing cultivators to focus on their progress, were sheltered under their blades when Demonic Beasts and renegade cultivators arose.

And so heads were bowed and limbs sent aquaking at the sight of the fast-moving cultivator.

All this, Zhao Wan ignored as he moved through destroyed villages and outposts, stopping only to purchase ready-made sustenance from farmwives and village heads before moving on. No cries for help or requests for his superior strength were proffered or offered in the wake of the disaster.

On the other hand, when Zhao Wan came across signs of a massive green snake, disturbed from its rest deeper in the wilderness, he did not hesitate to dispatch it. A single sword blow was all that was required to decapitate the creature before he dug out its spirit stone and skinned the beast sufficiently to acquire a series of meat chunks for sustenance.

The next village he came across was more than happy to divert some of their men to inform the previous village and begin the process of harvesting the remainder of the massive being. The bounty of spirit meat would not only restore physical bodies faster, it would add much needed protein to their diets—a rare enough occurrence, especially after the loss of much of their aquaculture.

Though Zhao Wan noted the minor threads of gratitude that arose from his acts, he dismissed concerns for them. While it was, theoretically, possible to live a life without such interactions or concerns, he knew he had decades left of exploration and understanding to achieve before he could grasp the complexities of the karmic path.

Others, like the Buddhist monks in the various temples who mixed cultivation and religion, might seek a resolution of such karmic balances or an achievement of immortality via growth and enlightenment of the soul; but such methods were slow and as prone to failure as the search for a dao.

No, in Zhao Wan's case, he chose a quicker path.

He sought to understand enough of the karmic weft to render the threads that bound him miniscule and thin. Understanding such threads and the burdens of their obligation, he would then separate them with his blade, shearing through it all like a farmer and his sheep.

In this way, he would be able to both interact with the world that existed while clearing himself of the debts one gathered by such interactions. It would be faster and less prone to distraction than other karmic daos.

When the sun began to set, Zhao Wan found himself tens of li from his original starting position. A racing horse could not have been faster than his journey, and not once had he caught sight of Shan Lin nor gained a hint of his presence. Content that he had left the man behind, Zhao Wan searched for a place to rest, his journey having taken him past the usual stopping points and resting areas that dotted the imperial highways.

Spotting a lean-to in the distance, one that was still intact, Zhao Wan at first considered himself fortunate. A small glow emanated from the building however, and to his chagrin as he neared, he noted the presence of another individual already inhabiting the location.

Annoyed and upset, he stomped over to stand before the Elder, who had a large pot of soup boiling, various pieces of thinly-sliced meat and vegetables floating within. The fragrant soup, filled with pieces of bitter melon, wild roots, and herbs and berries, caused Zhao Wan's stomach to rumble, though his sudden hunger was insufficient to distract him from his annoyance.

"What are you doing here?" he said. "How did you get here before me?"

Shan Lin grinned, hooking a thumb over his shoulder. "There's a small side road that cuts through the surroundings and shortens the journey. I would have told you of it this morning, but you were gone when I woke."

"I do not need your help."

"So you've said." Silence filled the small lean-to before Shan Lin raised the ladle. "Soup?" He gestured to the bowls beside him, filled with cooked glass noodles. "I have enough for both of us."

Zhao Wan snarled, then turned aside, moving toward a corner of the lean-to that bordered the sloping wall. He cleared the ground, finding some new and dry brush to set on the floor to insulate himself against the earth, and laid out a reed mat before sitting down. All the while, the smell from the cooking pot filled the surroundings.

Sitting by himself, noting that there was but a single fireplace in this simple travelers' shelter, his stomach grumbling its protest over the lack of food, he brooded. Eventually, Zhao Wan stood and extracted a chunk of snake meat from his storage ring, using a stick to spit the item.

"I need space to cook this," he said. "If you will trade, I have Spirit Beast meat from a snake I slew to share."

Shan Lin nodded agreeably, shifting the pot such that there was space for the skewer. Together, the pair sat on opposite sides of the fireplace, the smoke slowly drifting upward. Food shared and traded, a simple commercial transaction.

It should not create any major problems. It would not. So Zhao Wan convinced himself. If he could not get rid of the man, he would at least ensure that their journey together had the least amount of impediments to his own ascension.

He eyed the older man, the tall Elder offering another bright smile, one that seemed filled with a joke that only he understood.

***

"How long?" Zhao Wan asked the next morning after breakfast.

The pair were walking along the road, the older man leading the way. If Zhao Wan was forced to spend time with the other, he would at least make use of Shan Lin's greater knowledge of the terrain.

"Depends. If we use my recommended route, I would say about three days," Shan Lin said. "At an easy pace, of course. I could fly it faster, but flight in this region is not recommended."

Not that he could, but Zhao Wan had to ask, "Why not?"

"Crows," Shan Lin said. "Not strong, but numerous." He tilted his head toward the sky, searching for them and finding nothing. "It's been quiet since the flood, but you never know when they'll be back. They are a real murder[5]."

"Three days then. That is good." Zhao Wan adjusted the angle of his sword hilt, his eyes never stopping in one place for long. Focusing entirely on the conversation was dangerous, especially as they traveled farther from the seat of power.

Though the Shen kingdom was not entirely wild, unlike some of the border provinces or even the no-man's-land between some nations at times, the continual appearance of Demonic and

---

[5] Pun jokes are weird, especially since a part of me still has them talking in Chinese. So while this works in English, it makes no sense in Chinese. Or vice-versa.

Spirit Beasts in the wilderness ensured that the gaps between villages were never entirely safe.

It was why the existence of sects, many whose areas of residence were away from the cities that mortals congregated within, was encouraged. Their presence and their need to be supplied with simple mortal produce ensured that they continually hunted down and looked after the very roads that the pair walked upon. Adding in the imperial patrols, a degree of stability could be created for peripheral settlements and allow the continual expansion of civilization.

"That is, if we don't stop to help or are requested to aid any of the villagers we pass by."

"I will not be doing that."

"I understand." Shan Lin fell silent for another half dozen steps. "On the other hand, I will."

"Then we will part there." Zhao Wan could not help but smile a little.

"You don't have to look that happy. Hurts my feelings."

"Not a concern."

"You must be a lot of fun at parties," Shan Lin said.

"I do not go to them much." Then, as though it mattered not, Zhao Wan added, "I am not invited to many anyway."

"Somehow, I am not surprised."

Taking that criticism in stride, Zhao Wan kept walking. The silence was soon interrupted by Shan Lin singing, choosing a poem about the coming of spring to belt out as he walked along. His voice was loud, echoing along the road but harmonious at least.

Lips pursed, Zhao Wan chose not to tell the man to be silent. He would accept the annoyance, if nothing else than to end the conversation. Head lowered, he sped up a tiny bit, allowing his spiritual sense to expand outward to keep watch for potential trouble even as he extracted the scroll from the Patriarch. It was about time to study this new technique and see what exactly the Thousand Miseries really was.

Chapter 7

"Seven Demonic Beasts. Four Spirit Beasts. One in the Core Formation stage or equivalent." Zhao Wan sighed as they made camp that evening. "Is your singing a martial technique to agitate that many creatures?'

Shan Lin let out a long laugh, slapping Zhao Wan on the shoulder. The pair were seated in a sloping clearing, one they had chosen to occupy when they realized that the last outpost of civilization Shan Lin had meant to use had been entirely destroyed by a landslip. "Not at all. They just understand good music."

"Probably why they were so angry."

"It's common, really." When Zhao Wan did not look convinced, the Forgotten Vale elder explained. "After a disaster, the chi of the surroundings areas is disturbed, as is the environment. These creatures are more agitated and are moving from one zone to the next in search of new grounds to reside within. This can be dangerous, so I sing."

"Sing."

"Yes. Those that are likely to create problems for the villagers are attracted. Those that aren't will ignore us." He tapped his two sword breaker hilts by his side, the pair of weapons layered on top of another on his left hip. Beside the pair, two fires were crackling merrily in separate makeshift fire pits, spits hung over them with choice cuts roasting slowly, releasing the delectable smells of crackling skin and dripping fat into the surroundings. "The rest make good eating."

That did bring an interesting question to mind, and Zhao Wan let his gaze drift to Shan Lin's armband. "Your storage band is very large. Much larger than most I've come across."

"Jealous?" Grinning wide, Shan Lin shook his head. "I can put in a good word, if you ask."

Zhao Wan shook his head, not willing to let the man tie a knot of obligation that way.

Knowledge, however, was much less concerning. "Who made it?"

"Eh, if I told you, he'd kill me." Then he grinned, though it was a little tighter than Zhao Wan would expect for a true joke. "It's not someone from the main sects anyway."

"A heretic?"

Shan Lin shrugged. "If you had to categorize him, I guess." The older man stroked his mustache, a small smile on his lips. "You'll find, as you get older, that the line between orthodox and heretical and otherwise is much less firm than you would think."

Zhao Wan could only grunt in disagreement.

"You'll see." When Zhao Wan chose not to rise to the provocation, Shan Lin continued. "His dao is a strange one anyway. He's a blacksmith whose dao is of folded space. He seeks insight into the space between the metals he works. He believes that even when he strikes and compresses and heats and binds metals together, there is still more space. That it is the hammering strikes he wields that folds the metals into one another, compressing them. Shrinking that space.

"It's why, when you blend two metals together, they lose weight and size."

"They do?" Zhao Wan said, surprised.

"They do."

"Huh."

That kind of training, while Zhao Wan had seen others partake of it, was never something he had felt a desire to indulge in. He had his sword, his readings, and his study of karma. Let others do the hard work of sweating over forges or pill furnaces. So long as they were paid well, there were no issues with karmic threads. Commercial transactions, when fair to both parties, were the least onerous of interactions.

"So he has an understanding of this space that he finds between two metals he compresses together. And because of that, he can make storage items of greater strength than others?"

"Yes. He takes great amounts of metal and beats them for days on end. Strikes them until they become smaller, folding the space they compress into along with the space in his workshop. Eventually, both the armband and the space and his dao come together." Smiling ever so slightly, Shan Lin reached for the band around his upper arm. He worked it clear of his bicep and tossed it to Zhao Wan. "Here."

The younger cultivator's hands reached to catch the armband, fingers splayed. He felt it land in both hands and was grateful a moment later that he had used both hands. For as easy as the other man had made it seem to carry and toss the item, it was incredibly heavy and dense. So much so that it sent Zhao Wan tumbling over the back of his stump, not having expected the difference in weight.

Without thinking, he kept the fall going, rolling and coming to his feet smoothly. He was already shifting the armband to one hand, pouring chi into his body to strengthen it even as Shan Lin rose and brought his sword breaker sweeping down at Zhao Wan's head.

Zhao Wan stepped and twisted, pivoting on his back foot to dodge the attack by inches. Then, with his free hand, he struck, stabbing a pair of fingers into the meaty part of his attacker's arm, in between the bones into the pressure point in the middle of his appendage.

The attack forced Shan Lin's hand to spasm, the heavy sword breaker falling to the ground. Zhao Wan finished his retreat, skipping farther back. Yet he noted that Shan Lin had not followed up his attack beyond the first motion, instead standing there with a wide grin.

"What was that about?" Zhao Wan said coldly.

"A test, of course. And a lesson."

"For who?"

"Me, obviously. It was enlightening."

Zhao Wan glowered and hefted the armband. He was almost tempted not to give it back, but theft was a damaging karmic thread, one that would tie him to the other in this life or the next. No, he would not do that to himself. Though…

Turning the storage band around in his hand, he eyed the swirling patterns etched into the metal armband, the way the colors shifted and twisted, the weight and density of the item that was incongruous with its size and the subtle pressure of the dao that imposed itself on him and reality.

It was clear that Shan Lin had not been lying. The armband had been made with a unique space dao, one unlike anything Zhao Wan had come across. It was stronger than those he carried on his fingers, but also had a greater drawback.

"Everything you put in here… the weight isn't reduced, is it?" he asked.

"Not at all. Strange, is it not? How other daos make the weight disappear?"

"Strange that this one doesn't."

"A matter of perception." Then Shan Lin grinned as though he had made a big joke.

Hesitating only for a moment more, Zhao Wan tossed back the armband. "Don't do that again. Next time, I might not stop."

"Heard and understood."

As he took a seat beside the other man, Zhao Wan could not help but note that the other cultivator had not promised not to repeat his attack.

Damn eccentrics.

***

Warning talismans strung around the campground, formation flags set around his body as he cultivated, Zhao Wan could not help but consider that for all his complaints, Shan Lin had been generous in his sharing of the bounty. Not that they hadn't both taken part in the fights, but Zhao Wan would not have attempted to draw those monsters to him.

In the meantime, as he cultivated, he reassessed his core and his soul, testing the strings that led outward from his soul. They were more numerous than his ability to count, stacked upon one another in a way that defied physical sense. He could run his mental-spiritual fingers through them, feeling their density and weight, but it would have been impossible for any true thread in reality to be layered in this manner.

And yet...

He sensed them. Noted the differences that had occurred. Some threads had faded, grown feather-thin. Others had thickened, coming to the forefront of his senses. He knew, from past experiences, that these often denoted births and deaths, individuals he had accumulated a debt to. Many in past lives that he might interact with now—or in the future. Or not at all, if he cut these threads apart now.

The cultivation exercise he used, the senses he spread out, they were the methods of fortune-tellers and fate-twisters. Unlike those charlatans—for the future was a complicated, twisted mess no human could reliably foretell or manipulate—Zhao Wan's efforts were more focused.

He might attempt to twist his own fate, but it was to reduce the burden of his karma. He had no desire to manipulate a foreseen future beyond the choices he made in the present. Foretelling was an entire branch of magic he had no truck with, though he was grateful for their techniques.

Tonight, he undertook the regular review of his karmic burden, overseeing the threads that had grown and changed. Most were wispy, barely more present than a cobweb. These came from the simple act of existence, the continued use and purchase of everyday goods.

In truth, Zhao Wan was not even sure if these threads could be considered karmic debts. How could there be a debt when commerce was done, goods made and paid for, and a balanced agreement was achieved? Certainly a coin to a beggar for a candle, the purchase of a bundle of firewood from hungry children might change their fate. But his transactions were, by design, none of those forms.

And yet, here they were.

What, then, did the existence of these threads mean? Was the very act of existence, of living, of transacting in one manner or another with another human a guarantee of a connection, however tenuous? Or were these threads he sensed not so much a karmic debt but a thread of fate and a mark of a connection made? Where each interaction tugged and pushed, diverted the pathway of another's life?

Perhaps these connections were not so much of fate and karma, but of social consequence? Did he sense and feel not the threads of heavenly fate but human connection? Each being that stood under the stars drew breath together, burdened the world and lifted humanity. Were these threads then just the fabric of society, binding him tight with each interaction?

If so, perhaps the hermits and ascetics were right.

Today, additional threads, tenuous and light, had formed. He knew not the faces, knew not the individuals, and yet they were numerous and varied in their thickness. Some were significantly thicker than he expected, almost as though…

"Ah. The lives we saved." It had to be. Knock-on effects from the creatures they had fought, the beasts they had killed. "*Hun dan.*"

Zhao Wan let his mind relax after speaking the curse. It was frustrating that even a good and mercenary deed could cause such a change. A flicker of gratitude for Shan Lin forcing the battles. After all, he avoided such action himself and would never have come across such a change without the other.

It helped to clarify aspects of his own existence and path.

In time, he would have to cut these threads, as he had so many others. He wondered briefly if they might be easier to part. Others of the same weight had been simple, the threads formed from commercial interactions, from missives and words spoken in passing. Minor interactions with those from his sect or his time as a mortal.

Perhaps, if he sliced just right, they would part, and he would hurt less in freeing himself. With that thought, he rubbed his stomach, feeling the ghostly pain of his earlier form. It had faded in the past few days, the damage done to his body healing under the constant flow of chi from his dantian. Yet he could sense the growing thread between him and Shan Lin as they interacted.

Damn that man for insisting on coming. Bless him.

Now, wasn't that a common refrain of his life? Unable to help himself, Zhao Wan laughed softly before he exited the cultivation exercise. It was time to return to studying the Hundred Delights and A Thousand Miseries sensing technique. After all, there were only a few days left.

Chapter 8

The ruins of the former city stood revealed before them, half-submerged by the flood waters that had washed down and been trapped within the valley. An old stream that had run alongside the village had overflown, creating the temporary lake, while the exit out of the valley between low hills in the southeast lay clogged. Wood and branches made the majority of the blockage, though mud and stone had helped clog the edges such that only a trickle of water now escaped.

"Why would they build a city in such a horrible location?" Zhao Wan muttered, squatting low to stare at the water lapping dozens of feet below him. At the same time, he allowed his senses to expand.

The Hundred Delights and A Thousand Miseries technique unrolled as well, his sense of smell sharpening with each breath. He could not help but wrinkle his nose at the smells of the world around him. His own clothing—mildly mildewed and sweat-clogged—and Shan Lin's, sword oil and rusting metal, drying wood and damp hemp the first to arrive.

Then the ever-present smell of dung, trekked through on the paths, and the touch of blood from the beasts they had killed. Grass and mud churned afresh, rotting flesh and crumbling bone. Old stone and crumbling mortar, stagnant water and the fungi that grew from it.

All of it revolting to the extreme.

The damn technique had been aptly named the Hundred Delights and A Thousand Miseries.

Emphasis on miseries.

"They didn't. They put themselves up against the rock cliff there—the one made of schist— but there had been an opening all about." Shan Lin pointed at the ground beneath their feet. "These hills here are not natural."

"What made them?" Zhao Wan asked, using this time to probe for more information and distract himself from the ongoing assault on his senses.

Shan Lin shrugged. "Unknown. It was what Elder Tung was trying to ascertain when we learnt about these ruins."

"How did that happen?" Zhao Wan rubbed his nose hard and released the cultivation exercise. If there were clues to be had, they were hidden under the lake. He stood and walked along the top of the hill toward the blockage.

"Some of the villagers had mentioned their presence. There were a few towers that stood above the crust"—Shan Lin gestured—"though most were hidden by the earth. They'd used the stones from the towers for their buildings, but a recent shifting in the earth had seen more uncovered. Along with it, some minor nuisances.

"They asked for our help, and when the inner sect members came to deal with them, they found the city. After killing the *jiangshi* and laying them to rest, they reported the incident and their findings and Elder Tung sought to learn more about the city."

Zhao Wan frowned, looking back at the Elder. "That doesn't make sense. Why would he try to learn about the hills when the ruins were new? How did he know the hills were even worth looking into?"

"Oh, the ruins weren't hard to pin down once we learnt about it. We do have a library," Shan Lin said coldly. "Older records indicated the founding of the city a hundred and eighty years ago. We even found indications of the taxes they had paid to us that stopped about nighty-seven years ago." The older man shook his head, a little amused as Zhao Wan continued to carefully pick his way around bushes along the top of the hill. "None of its presence was a problem. The issue was the change in geography."

"A whole city disappearing was not an issue?" Zhao Wan said.

"You obviously are not used to the borders." Shan Lin shrugged. "We have no indications of the final reason, but mortals die out here. When Demonic Beasts and humanity abut, one or the other falls." A slight smile then. "Mostly the demons."

"But not always."

"But not always."

A long exhalation by Zhao Wan as he reviewed the soggy ground, the earth having washed away portions of the valley to reveal the village that had been hidden by time and destructive cultivation techniques. The loss of the city was no act of nature, though whether it had been caused by Demonic or Spirit Beast or a human cultivator, he had no idea. After all, he was no earth element cultivator, no detective or archaeologist. He was more concerned about the future than the past.

Small stones were all that remained of the lower half of buildings. The crumbled, pressed earth retaining walls and the foundation stones spoke of the presence of previous structures. In other spots where other buildings would have been, should have been, the ground lay empty but for the still water of the impromptu lake. No sign of a residence, earthen walls and clay tiles having washed away.

Finally making his way to within a quarter li of the blockage, Zhao Wan squatted again to eye it. His lips thinned as he considered his next move, turning only a little when Shan Lin came to stand by his shoulder, arms crossed.

"You know, that's a bad idea." He gestured down the hill at the blockage. "Letting out so much water at once, it'll cause problems downstream."

"Any villages?" Zhao Wan said.

"None that are occupied right now. We had to evacuate those a while ago due to the flooding. It will eventually join the Mao River, then the outflow won't make a difference compared to what's already being added. The dikes and locks should be able to handle the overflow."

"Then there's no problem."

"Except for everything that washes away or gets damaged. Just because no one is living there right now doesn't mean there won't be damage," Shan Lin said heatedly.

Zhao Wan considered his words, looking at the small lake. He stood up as he eyed the lapping water, the way it hid so much. "Do you swim well?"

"Decently." Shan Lin relaxed.

"I don't."

Drawing and spinning at the same time, Zhao Wan sent a blade of energy arcing through the air, striking the water and cutting through it. When it impacted the blockage and earth leading out from the hills that had been formed around the village, an explosion of water and dirt occurred. Mud, branches, and leaves rained down on the pair, bouncing off their aura defenses to leave them untouched.

A moment later, the crack of the blockage giving way fully echoed through the surroundings, followed soon after by the rush of water as the earth and wood was washed away. The trickle became a deluge, and each moment, additional portions of the makeshift dam washed away.

Sheathing his sword, Zhao Wan cocked his head at Shan Lin, who was glaring at him.

"Shall we make dinner? It'll not drain for a few hours at the least."

"Damn it, Ah Wan! You can't just do things like that."

"I am certain that the past has shown that I can."

"You… you…" Waving his hands ineffectually, Shan Lin turned back to the water, clenching his fist and jerking it upward. Blockages of earth sprang upward, helping to slow the sudden outflow a little. It did not last long.

Zhao Wan paid no attention to the Forgotten Vale elder, already planning out lunch. As he'd said, it would be hours before the valley drained. If not longer.

***

It was longer.

Zhao Wan might be a sword saint in the making, but he certainly was no engineer. The amount of water captured by the valley had been significantly greater than he had expected. He had to return to the blockage twice more to strike at the ground, digging deep trenches into the river floor to allow the escape of the remaining water.

Even after all that, the next morning saw a still-muddy, pond-filled land. A low mist had arisen, leaving the ruins shrouded in a damp softness that pervaded the senses. Now that the water was no longer hiding the evidence, the overpowering flow of water chi a minor trickle, Zhao Wan noticed the presence of another chi signature in the air.

"There's necrotic yin chi down there," Zhao Wan said, his fingers tracing the pommel of his sword.

"Concentrated too." A finger rose, and Zhao Wan was surprised to note the lines and wrinkles on Shan Lin's hand. "That way, in particular. I think the water overturned the cemetery."

Zhao Wan narrowed his eyes, staring at the supposed cemetery in mild concern. An overabundance of yin chi—often found in cemeteries and other grave sites—often led to the rising of the undead. The jiangshi were the most common kind, the hopping vampires mostly mindless monsters of hunger and rage. They were drawn to the pulsing yang energy of the living, wishing to consume what they no longer naturally produced.

In bad cases, where yin chi concentrated in high degrees, the jiangshi that rose were stronger and sometimes smarter. Rather than mindless creatures driven by hunger and animated by the yin energies of the world, an escaped ghost might inhabit their bodies.

In such cases, the resulting jiangshi was no longer a mindless vampiric monster or a wandering ghost but an unholy amalgamation of the two. Creatures like that had an intrinsic ability to control other jiangshi, able to motivate the hopping vampires to work for them in their attacks against wildlife and villagers. Even more dangerously, if they managed to procure a powerful enough yang-chi source, they could empower themselves and live in spreading zones of yin-aspected land.

Dead zones that killed vegetation and individuals within. To ensure that such yin-energy zones grew, the monstrous jiangshi would send out its minions to acquire more living creatures, slaughter them, and leave their bodies to rot on the borders, thus increasing the amount of yin energy present.

In short, jiangshi were a danger. Especially during the fall when the hungry ghost month arose. It was the job of every cultivator, every sect to destroy such creatures long before they became a problem. Or they would face, once more, hordes of the undead. Or so said the stories. The last such horde had been centuries ago and only spoken of via records and the occasional Nascent Spirit Elder who had survived that time.

"I'll check," Shan Lin said, unsheathing his weapons.

"Why go now?" Zhao Wan said, pointing upward. "The sun has not fully risen. Let the mist burn off. When the monsters are weakest, we can fight them. If there are any."

"Are you afraid of some minor jiangshi? I was fighting them when I was a Body Cultivator!" Shan Lin boasted.

"With a peach sword, surely. I carry none. And I see no point in expending energy when a little patience will ease our troubles."

"And I'd rather finish the job now!" So saying, Shan Lin stalked off.

Zhao Wan found himself frowning, watching the impatient older man leave. Some people never grew up, never gave up on acting without thought. And while impatience was understandable among children and the young, it was much less attractive amongst the elderly.

Shaking his head, Zhao Wan turned away and returned to their temporary encampment. He stoked the fire, prodding at the coals, and searched nearby for kindling to toss on it. There wasn't much in terms of dry fuel around, the occasional shower after the flash flood having kept things soaked. Still, they had managed to find a few handfuls last night and he had kept some for this morning.

After tossing the leaves and small sticks on the fire, he turned toward the nearest copse of trees. A short journey there and back had him return with a few armfuls of lumber, some of it newly broken off, much of it from deadfalls washed aside and held up during the flood. He threw those next to the fire, spreading them around so that they would dry as the kindling sparked and lit, burning with a small flame. He picked up other branches they had set next to the fire last night and added a few to the burgeoning flames.

Once they had caught, then and only then did he look back to where Shan Lin fought. In the mist-filled valley, shadows moved and the dull crack and thud of sword breakers impacting bone and dried flesh echoed. The occasional human cry—never raised in distress but in surprise or, more often, disgust—rose from within the valley too.

Zhao Wan listened, then expanded his senses, breathing in the stink of the dead and dying. He made a face, though he made sure to keep the sensory exercise running even as he turned back to the flame. He made no offer of help. That would be a complication he did not need. Instead, he commented under his breath as he fed more sticks to his flame.

"Impatient fool."

And all the while, as he started a second breakfast and a pot of water for tea, he kept the new sensory art running. He smelled and listened, content to wait for additional dangers.

Chapter 9

Shan Lin stomped back up the hill, his robes splattered with mud and bone. Both sword breakers were held away from his body as dried gristle and mud slowly dripped from them. The mist had mostly burnt away, leaving the remnant buildings further exposed. In spots, yawning chasms where cold rooms had been dug into the ground were present, flanked by the remnants of stone walls and flagstones over the kitchens and entrances.

This was an outpost village, requiring both farming and subsistence off the takings from the nearby forest, whether it be lumber, meat, or fungi. So far out from the normal trade routes and kingdom patrols, the village also had an outer wall, though like the remainder of the village, only portions remained.

The cemetery Shan Lin had returned from was on the outskirts of the wall, near where the outflow had been. The constant churn of water and the unnatural state of the hills that surrounded the village had stripped the land even more than the rest of the village, leading to the rising of the creatures. Or so Zhao Wan theorized.

"You could have helped!" Shan Lin growled as he threw himself down beside the cackling fire.

A pot of rice porridge was boiling away merrily, the rice slowly breaking down. Small portions of salted fish and fatty, preserved sausages had been added to give the porridge body while nearby, a heaping portion of freshly picked fungi sat by the side.

"You could have waited."

"The jiangshi were awake now. Better to deal with them when they're coming at you, rather than digging them up from their hiding places." Shan Lin sniffed. "Unless you intended to spend the day doing that."

Zhao Wan hesitated, then inclined his head. He chose not to bother discussing his own reticence, the choice of adding karmic debts—even to the dead whose bodies had been disturbed—to the entire thing. Better to let it lie for now.

"Well. What did you intend to see here anyway?" Shan Lin said.

Zhao Wan shrugged. "We will have to see, won't we?" He nodded to the food, adding the mushrooms to the porridge and giving it a good stir.

In the silence, Shan Lin took out a cloth and began the process of cleaning his weapons, wiping them first with the rag before switching to plain water to finish the cleaning process. Once he was done, he extracted another cloth to dry the rectangular blades, being careful to move his fingers around the notches. Once the blades were properly dry, he pulled out a small bottle of sword oil, using another cloth to rub in the oil. No need to hone the weapons—solid bars of metal that they were, a notch or two were of no concern for their functionality.

"Food's ready." Zhao Wan called, glancing at Shan Lin's oil-covered hands. "I'll put some aside."

"I'm not fussy," Shan Lin said, making grabbing motions with his hands when he'd set down the sword breaker and cloth. "It's not like I'm dipping my hands in the meal."

Zhao Wan hesitated, then nodded. "Of course."

The meal was finished quickly, both cultivators wanting to proceed to the goal of their journey. After banking the fire, Zhao Wan covered the pot of rice with a lid and set it on a nearby flat stone before giving his utensils and bowl a quick rinse.

He glanced at Shan Lin, who was still happily eating, and shrugged. Zhao Wan had not wanted his presence anyway. Though, he had to admit, Shan Lin's company had made the journey a lot less boring. Dismissing the matter, he chose to walk down the hill, avoiding muddy patches and dirty puddles.

When he reached the bottom, Zhao Wan walked the perimeter of the old village. His eyes drifted over the broken-down packed earth and stone walls, searching for signs of battle or destruction. Eventually, he made his way to the overturned cemetery, eyeing the formation flags that had been buried around the perimeter. He felt the twisting of environmental chi as he stared at the flags, the bands of power forming between each flag to lower the ambient yin chi and capture the yang chi streaming down from the heavens.

"I'll carve some more permanent formations soon," Shan Lin said from behind Zhao Wan.

"You're a formation master?" Zhao Wan said, surprised.

"I would never call myself a master." Shan Lin shrugged his broad shoulders. "But in a small sect like ours, you have to learn a little of everything to get by."

"Then what would you call yourself?"

"Just a small sect Elder." The older man grinned. "I do a little of everything. I can't fight. Not like the Guardian. I can't teach, not like Elder Tung. I'm not wise like the Patriarch. Or smart like Physician Gu." He tapped his chest. "I just do everything else they don't. A few formations here and there, some apothecary brewing, teaching, patrolling." He grinned. "I'm good at raising walls and helping the villagers though."

"Is that the path of your dao then?" Zhao Wan asked.

"The dao of many things and not much good at any?" Shan Lin let out an uproarious laugh. "Oh, what a dao would that be." He laughed and laughed, and it forced a smile from Zhao Wan at the incongruity of it. "But no, I'm just a seeker of small changes."

"A… what?"

This time, Shan Lin chose not to answer. Instead, he pointed at the cemetery. "The smell, the sense of decaying chi. It came from within there, but it was just the jiangshi. With them gone, it is dispersing now. Don't you think?"

Zhao Wan continued to stare at the older man until he let out a long sigh. Obviously Shan Lin was choosing not to speak of his dao. Letting his newly learnt sensing technique expand once more, Zhao Wan drew in a deeper breath. He gagged a little at the smell of mud and still water, of the overturned graves and the shattered remnants of the rotting jiangshi—their decomposition sped up as the last of the animating yin energy left them.

He breathed, cycling air in and out of his lungs, tasting the chi and picking apart the various smells. Zhao Wan cycled through the experience, fighting down the bouts of nausea and gagging that threatened to overwhelm him.

Practicing this technique in the Verdant Green Waters, where the mountain air was clean and smelled of flowers and mountain shrubbery, would be much preferrable.

Eventually though, he managed to pick apart the odors sufficiently that he could push down the sensing technique, letting the scents fade into the background again. He noted, idly, that his sense of smell still seemed to be overly sensitive, though Zhao Wan was uncertain if it was perhaps his imagination.

In either case…

"You are right. I sense the necrotic energy fading. It was likely the jiangshi. Your formation flags, I believe, will eventually drive it all away," he said.

"Told you." Shan Lin smoothed out his mustache with a pair of fingers. "I should make one more walk, now that the sun is out. Make sure they're all gone."

So saying, the Elder walked through the formation. He let out a little shiver as he passed through the borders, and Zhao Wan followed. The change in energy as he traveled through the formation was like a cold wind blowing over his skin as the gathered yin energy was dispersed into the environment.

Walking beside Shan Lin, Zhao Wan eyed the simple—and in a few cases, elaborate—headstones that dotted the landscape, many of them overturned or toppled, a few elaborate tombs sunk into the earth. Not many of those, which wasn't surprising for a border town. As he looked around, movement in the corner of his eyes had him flinching backward. Only to stop after he had retreated a few steps when he realized the movement was that of a censer held by the Forgotten Vale Elder, the censer swinging back and forth as sage and other herbs were burnt.

"Purifying?" Zhao Wan said.

"Yes. I'll burn some hell paper[6] later."

The pair kept walking, the smoke from the censer boiling outward and further dissipating the necrotic chi in the atmosphere. More than that though, it helped with the pervasive smell of churned mud and algae and the lingering smell of rotting corpses, though few enough were found.

In the center, a fire burned. The jiangshi corpses were on fire, piled up by Elder Shan, such that they could be cleaned and cleansed. No surprise that the other man had gathered the corpses and started the fire, even if it further despoiled the bodies. The fire ate the yin chi of the ex-jiangshi, transforming them into yang as the bodies fueled the flames. Sacrilegious it might be, but it was necessary too. All they could

---

[6] Also known as ghost paper or spirit money or joss paper, it's paper "fake" money burnt to help the spirit pay for their afterlife and ensure they're sufficiently taken care of. There are three colors, with the copper / yellow for new or unknown ghosts.

do was pay for the damage later with hell money and hope the owners had passed on to the next cycle of rebirth.

Even though the older man might have tried to do a thorough job, in the dark, once the creatures stopped moving, and in the heat of the battle, he had missed more than one portion. Zhao Wan spotted the occasional crushed limb, split torso, and head that had been missed.

"You said this village had disappeared decades ago, did you not?" the young cultivator said.

Shan Lin nodded. "I did. Why?"

"The bodies should have rotted away already," Zhao Wan said.

Or at least, rotted significantly more than what he noted in the disparate body parts. Without at least a mostly complete body, animation of the hopping vampires was incredibly rare. So there should have been fewer jiangshi, fewer corpses to animate than the number of limbs he counted. Either that or the villagers were severely mutated.

He sniffed, smelling a more powerful, stronger source. He found it under a crushed tombstone, one that was still partly submerged in a dirty pond. The tomb was a wreck, but once had been done up in an elaborate manner such that it looked like a small mansion. The corpse had tumbled into the headstone then, its movement suspended by its hard approach, crashed into the sunken earth beneath. The gravestone itself had toppled over soon after, crushing the body and hiding the corpse.

Zhao Wan stood before the wreck, lips pursed in thought. He lifted the gravestone easily, tossing the stone slab aside with one hand before he squatted beside the unmoving corpse. Frowning, he reached out sideways. A stick flew from the ground to land in his hand, pulled to him via chi tendrils he had extended. Using his recently acquired tool, he prodded the body. He disregarded the wide, smashing blows that had crushed bone and ripped apart dried flesh. Instead, he focused on the older wounds, on the remnant clothes on the body. He let his gaze roll over the corpse before Zhao Wan stood and turned to the side, eyes drifting back to the village again then down to the body.

"This corpse, it's recent. No more than a half a year," Zhao Wan said. The damn flood made guessing difficult, since he was uncertain how being waterlogged changed the timing or destruction of the body. "And it was not buried, I think. It was left here after it was killed." A hand pointed at the cut on its ragged throat. "How many?"

"How many what?"

"How many jiangshi did you destroy?"

"Forty-eight. All adults."

"Hun dan[7]!"

---

[7] Equivalent of bastard

Shan Lin nodded. "It explains some of the disappearances."

"What disappearances?" Zhao Wan asked.

Shan Lin was quick to explain about mentions of disappearing mortals in the villages, an increase in deaths. They'd thought it was a Spirit Beast or Demonic Beast preying upon the villages. Nothing too concerning, especially as they'd sent out inner sect cultivators to deal with them.

Till the flood of course.

"This shirt. It's high-grade silk. So's the undershirt," Zhao Wan said, pointing. "Not the usual fare around here."

"No, it's not. Nor is his hairstyle… I think there were others. Different looking. They must have been bringing villagers from far away here."

No need to ask which they. Neither knew.

Yet.

Zhao Wan continued his investigation in silence, hurrying through the graveyard. There was no locus point, no section where the jiangshi could have been said to have risen. It didn't help that the fire burned the corpses, hiding where the battles might have been fiercest. All he had to go on were the imprints in the mud, and he was no tracker.

The cemetery had no further clues for him, just reiterations of the information already acquired. Zhao Wan left both the slow-moving Shan Lin and the cemetery to enter the village. His eyes darted from side to side as he took in the ruins, the empty, rutted streets, and deep pools of stagnant water.

Now that he was looking for it, he caught hints of recent settlement. A tent here. Pots and pans that were mostly unrusted. A shoe. Washed here perhaps, or left behind by accident? No buildings were rebuilt though, so whatever had happened here, it had been as a temporary encampment. Curiouser and curiouser.

It was dark by the time Zhao Wan had finished prodding and surveying the grounds. He had not even covered the whole village properly, instead spending time acquiring the unusual items, the newer ones, and setting them aside.

There was a mystery here, and he intended to unearth it. And in so doing, find the answer to who had harmed Elder Tung. Or so he hoped.

Chapter 10

Two days. It took Cheng Zhao Wan two days to admit—out loud—what he had, or should have, known from the very start of the entire process. After walking the village boundaries twice, the washed-out roadways and slow drying muddy ground thrice, enduring another rain shower and watching it wash away the signs of their own passing, and finally, stepping into and out of the various ruins, he admitted defeat.

"I can find no identifying traces of who was here or what they were up to. They could have been scholars reviewing the ruins or an army encampment or brigands or cultivators. But nothing that we have found points to any specific group," Zhao Wan said that afternoon. He pointed at the pile of former belongings he had extracted from the mud and ruins, eyebrows creased as his frustration leaked through his voice. "Unless you have noticed something I haven't in the trash."

"Not at all," Shan Lin said. "Investigations are really not something I excel in." He chuckled self-depreciatingly. "I'm more the Elder you call in to help when a wall falls or you need a dike built. Elder Tung is the one we went to for such things."

"Which might be why he's the one injured," Zhao Wan said.

"Might be." Shan Lin tilted his head. "I'm surprised you have nothing like that though. I thought you Verdant Green Waters Sect Elders prized the learning and flexibility of being a 'proper' sect."

Zhao Wan sighed. "We do. But because of my path, I chose simple assignments. I never needed to study elaborate methods of investigation. Spirit or Demonic Beasts are not hard to locate. Expeditions by Elders required only that I wielded my sword well. Even guard duty was rather straightforward." He grimaced. "The few times I had to deal with wilier opponents, I was often partnered with others who had the right skills."

"So you never learned to investigate properly."

"No. Though…" He gestured down at the village, the muddy ground. "I wonder if even the most skilled investigator could learn anything after all this time and rain."

Shan Lin shrugged. The pair fell silent before the older cultivator asked, "Now what do you intend? I have another few days of carving to complete before the formation markers are ready."

He gestured toward the big stones he had pried from the walls of the buildings below, the enchantment still in the process of being inscribed, the formation lines being chipped away. There were five formation stones set next to one another, one for each of the major elements, and Shan Lin had finished carving two. By the side, the shattered remnants of three other stones lay, when enthusiasm and strength had seen to their destruction.

"I do not know," Zhao Wan said.

That was a lie. He did know. He just did not like to contemplate it. But when Shan Lin offered no additional aid, instead turning back to his carving, Zhao Wan admitted to himself that he might need to delve into the one skill he had that might lead him to his prey. Reluctant as he might be.

Another deep breath, then Zhao Wan bade farewell to the other elder. He received a grunt in return, before the cultivator traveled toward the nearby forest. His goal was within, brushing against the edges of his senses as they had camped and investigated.

***

The creature that stalked the forest, that had tested the boundaries of the formations the pair had set up late at night to protect themselves was wily. It only allowed itself to be sensed occasionally, its presence the slightest pressure on Zhao Wan's spiritual sense before it was gone. That pressure was so slight that the cultivator might have considered it his imagination if he had not been stalked by another big cat in the past. Now, the careful attention that unconsciously sharpened into a killing intent when his attention drifted was like a beacon to his paranoid feelings.

At first, Zhao Wan had considered whether the creature could be the source of the poison that had struck down Elder Tung. It would have been a simple and convenient explanation. Too simple. Too convenient. Zhao Wan held that option in mind, though he had little hope for it to be so.

Instead, he stalked the forest, drifting from branch to earth, across washed up dirt dams and soggy moss, his qinggong method running on the regular. Knowing that he was counter-stalking a wild creature of great cunning, and recalling the Patriarch's and Physician Gu's words, Zhao Wan concentrated on locking down his own scent.

As a cultivator, he sweated little, exuded the mortal stench even less. Yet less was not nothing, nor were his clothes and the rose water perfume he used on the insides of his wrist and the back of his neck without their own odor.

Learning to wield his aura in a way to contain such aromas, releasing them only when it was appropriate—when a strong wind blew and he was in the tree branches high above mostly—was a constant and wearing experience. More than once, Zhao Wan felt his control falter, the hardened barrier of his aura—a barrier modified by the simple aura umbrella technique used by his sect—becoming permissive once more.

There was, to Zhao Wan's chagrin, another major issue with containing one's scent. By locking down the flow of air around himself, carrying such smell with him, he not only concentrated it but also made it more difficult for himself to breathe. Too harsh a breath and he would pierce his own technique.

A frustrating conundrum.

On the first day, Zhao Wan never caught a glimpse of his prey. On the second, as his control grew better, he spotted his target once. A flash of movement in the corner of his eye, grey and white with small black spots. No larger than a human, though faster than any mortal.

After that, he didn't see it again for the next three days he spent in the forest, stalking the creature all hours of the day. Yet he knew it was still present, for the sharpened killing intent of the creature that tore at his spiritual sense and left surface scratches upon his soul flickered to life over and over again.

He had caught the Spirit Beast's attention, and now it played with him.

On the fourth day, Zhao Wan gave up. Other prey that he might have sought to use for his technique had long been driven away by the sharpened killing intent of the leopard. Left with no quarry, no clues of who might have camped in the village or the source of Elder Tung's poisoning, Zhao Wan released his frustration.

He struck and struck again, tearing apart the trees, toppling them with strikes of blade intent and chi. A single cut was all that was required to split trunks two-hands-span wide. A drop kick rent apart the earth, digging a wide trench. In a flurry of movement, Zhao Wan created a new clearing in the untouched, centuries-old forest.

After his rage had been spent on the defenseless vegetation, the cultivator sheathed his weapon and sat on a log, putting his head in his hands. He sat there in silence, allowing his breathing to deepen, for rage to calm and his senses to cool.

Minutes turned into hours, and corded muscles relaxed, his body slumping over as he leaned against the broken stump of a tree. His head lowered, his breathing low and slow, he did not move. As the sun set, the clearing grew colder faster than the surroundings, no trapped heat in the air to warm the surroundings.

In the distance, at the edge of the clearing, a shadow drifted. It had stalked the cultivator for days now, playing with him. Now, it allowed its presence to be sensed, relaxing its control of its aura. The figure in the clearing twitched once then stilled as the killing intent—so close that it was but a second of bounding away—brushed against its senses.

Then the figure that smelled of blood and sword oil, of broken grass and lives lost, stilled.

The shadow crept sideways, suppressing its aura and killing intent once more. It settled into the hunting mindset it had learned long ago, the mindset that allowed it to take down arrogant cultivators and powerful Spirit Beasts. It chose not to think about the final act, the moment when it pounced and clamped its teeth on its prey, but instead on the motions itself.

Even if it did not know the words, the beast understood the Dao. It understood *wu wei*, the process of taking action without doing so. When intent and action became one, such that the movement and the moment were effortless. It understood killing intent and wanting something so badly that, like clutching water too hard, one could lose what one grasped for. The beast followed its own dao, and in so doing, its steps covered the distance between the pair. It circled halfway over then crept ever closer, its spotted grey and white hide blending into the lengthening shadows of the evening.

Long minutes, so long that an incense stick would have burnt to ash and the ash itself be blown away, the leopard crawled closer. Until it was a half dozen feet away, a simple pounce for the powerful creature. Muscles tensed and released and the monster soared through the air, its killing intent never spiking, its mind clear of everything but the motion itself.

And the figure, slumped over until that moment, moved.

Too close to block, the man took the easiest option. Already slumped forward, Zhao Wan let himself fall forward. Holding onto his sword sheath as he did so, he rolled over the back of his neck and shoulder on the rough dirt before turning, hand on hilt.

Sword hand and sheath hand moved in opposite directions, the blade coming free with a hiss of flickering light and blade intent. Chi exploded from the drawn sword, catching the stalking cat who, having missed its prey, had leapt back toward the safety of the all-too-far trees.

The cut struck the cloud leopard on its back legs, slicing deep on the diagonal. It tore through the creature's defensive aura, toughened fur, and corded muscle to bite into vulnerable tendons and bone. A loud yowl arose from the creature as its initial jump was disrupted. Twisting in mid-air, the leopard landed on its injured back feet, the pair buckling a little. Already, Zhao Wan was standing, the blade moving in an intricate form that sent a blade storm of chi intent at the monster.

Chi sharpened, and the strong scent of blood and clouds intensified as the cloud leopard utilized its chi. Wounds along its legs healed a little, allowing it to dodge the incoming blade strikes. Bouncing from side to side, the cloud leopard chose not to fight but flee, seeking to lose the hunter in the wilderness.

But here, the great landscape of destruction left it with few areas to hide or alter course. No heights to change, no trees to leap off. Even throwing itself from side to side and, once, pouring sufficient strength into its footing to create a firm cloud to leap from, it was unable to flee the fast-moving crescent arcs of blade intent flying after it.

Injuries accumulated, striking the back of the creature and its initial wound. Impacts across skin and fur widened the original cut on its back legs. Damaged tendons gave way and the creature flopped to the ground, only to be bisected by a final blade strike.

Zhao Wan dashed forward then, blade raised to strike down the creature and behead it. A last-minute lunge saw the monster twist from the descending attack and clamp its mouth on an upraised arm still holding the sword sheath in hand.

Wooden sheath shattered, chi-empowered and sharpened fangs cracking crafted wood. Enchanted silk tore as fangs pierced through jade green robes to capture muscular arm. A wrench of the head threw Zhao Wan to the side, but even as he flew, his sword tracked the motion and line of the body. It cut down and across, slicing across neck and muscles.

By the time he landed, the headless corpse was spilling blood in the air tens of feet away. The head, still clamped around his arm, glared at him balefully for a moment before the life faded from the monster's eyes, leaving Zhao Wan standing there, victorious and injured.

After stabbing his sword into the earth, Zhao Wan sought to pry the head off his arm, cursing as he pulled finger-long fangs out of his limb. Blood gushed freely from the wounds even as he stored the head aside. He would extract the eyes, tongue, and fangs later—all items the apothecarist in his sect would desire. But that was for the future.

In the meantime, he had a wound to bandage, a body to bring back, and a ritual to perform.

Chapter 11

The headless corpse of the cloud leopard lay in the middle of the ruined village, its stomach slit, the entrails extracted. Beneath the entrails lay a large sheet of paper, a series of characters scribbled down the paper starting with the species of the slain, the time of its death, and the location of its death before additional information was added. Further information, drawn from the reading of the entrails and the creature's death, along with consultation of the fortune-telling book Zhao Wan had extracted, was written on the paper.

Standing a short distance away, frowning heavily and with great disapproval, was Shan Lin. He stared at the corpse, the damage and disfigurement that had been done to it, and the intense concentration Zhao Wan evidenced as he worked, environmental chi swirling around the entire process. Shan Lin cursed silently.

Fortune-telling came in many forms. The most benign were the Bazi, Yi Jing, Kau Cim, and palmistry[8] methods, for those only sought to see the overall flow of one's fate and fortune. Even then, such undertakings were fraught with danger, for the very act of fortune-telling could alter the course of the future. Furthermore, the constant use of such skills all throughout the kingdoms, by kings and farmers alike, ensured that no fortune stayed the same from moment to moment.

But there were darker, less civilized arts. Arts that came from outside the Middle Kingdom, that were practiced by the clans and other ethnic groups. That required the sacrifice of creatures and the concurrent drawing of energies—both yin and yang—to empower the divination. Such methods were more powerful and more reliable,

---

[8] Bazi is the four pillars method (uses time of birth to tell fortune), Yi Jing is otherwise known as the I Ching and uses various castings—coins, yarrow stalks, etc—compared to the book of fortunes, Kau Cim is the throwing of incense sticks from a bamboo cylinder and is for short-term fortunes, and palmistry is, well, palmistry.

for they also encouraged and solidified the future they sought. At the same time, by binding the future, they went against the dictates of heaven and the heavenly dao, an act that bordered on heresy itself.

Shan Lin found himself speaking up, his voice troubled. "Young man, I understand your impatience and desire for an answer. But to rebel against heaven's dictates—"

"Is what we do, as cultivators," Zhao Wan answered without looking up. "After all, the very act of seeking immortality is against the natural order."

"Even so, gaining their attention early is never a good idea. Do you not know that diviners rarely ascend, for the heavens seek their demise more than even ours?" Shan Lin said.

"Of course I do. And I'm no fool," Zhao Wan answered, his brush stilling at last as he came to the end of his paper. He stepped away, storing the writing implements in his storage ring. "I have no faith in the ever-turning whims of foretold futures and fickle fortunes. I only borrow some of their techniques."

"To do what?" Shan Lin asked.

"To find the thread that binds me to our prey." Then, to punctuate the end of the conversation, he clapped his hands together. Power poured from his limbs, filling the very air with his chi, the cut-edge sharpness of a blade surrounding them.

It caused Shan Lin to hesitate, for each moment, each breath felt as if he might breathe too deep and cut himself.

The air pulsed once, then again, before the chi came crashing down onto the paper and the body. It shone brightly, like the edge of a sword in midday sun. It blinded the older cultivator, forcing him to squint. Through half-closed eyes, he noticed that Zhao Wan shone, threads the color of blood and silver leading outward from his chest.

Threads of fate and karma, of obligation and debt. They pulsed with the lifeblood of the slain cloud leopard, with the darkness of the debt incurred. Light played along the edges of the threads as lines led in myriad directions, so many that Shan Lin felt nauseated from even watching them move.

"What is this?"

"My karma." Zhao Wan hushed him, his fingers rising and playing along the threads. He plucked at some of the larger, more prominent threads before discarding them, moving on. Sensing that his answer was insufficient, Zhao Wan continued to speak as he worked. "My master, back in the Sect." He traced a finger along a thread that was nearby, so faint it was almost non-existent. "The Patriarch, who I owe for watching over me." Then another, this one glittering and dark. "An old debt, brought to life. A lover, a mother, a life lost. One day, they shall be repaid, and repay my debts." He touched another thread, his voice growing dreamy. "This one comes and goes, as though its fate has yet to be chosen. Will it join mine, or will the piece be placed on another board? Not even the gods know yet."

Then he turned away, facing back the way they came. Fewer threads here, leading back to the sect. "The mortals we passed, that we influenced as we traveled through their lands." Numerous spider-thin threads, breaking even as Zhao Wan touched them with his glowing, sharp fingers. "Foolishly believing in obligation and duty, your Patriarch and Physician bind me to them with their gifts of technique and advice." A snarl in his voice as his fingers brushed the pair of lines, the thicker threads refusing to break so easily.

"And Elder Tung, who saved me, condemned me." A beat, as he plucked the thicker thread, nearly a finger-width across. He watched it vibrate; the edges barely frayed by the cutting edge of his fingers. Then, running his fingers along the vibrating thread, he turned, tracing sideways. "And there. There… our prey. The thread from him to his attacker, to me. Do you see it? Do you mark it? Can you see how the wheel turns, grinding us all beneath? We are but playthings for fate and karma, our desires nothing more than dreams meant to be cast aside…"

He laughed then, a painful, hiccupping laugh. Shan Lin's eyes widened as the light touched upon the threads, the cutting edge of Zhao Wan's chi tore and tore into the threads that bound him. Zhao Wan laughed, and cuts appeared across the exposed skin of his face and arms, slashing his robes as his aura reacted to his feelings, as he sought to free himself.

"Playthings, bound to one another. Do you not want to be free? I do."

"Enough! Boy, enough. This is not the way. You know it. Bound as you might be, as we might be, this is not the way!" Shan Lin roared.

"But I want… I need…" Zhao Wan hiccupped, coughed, then collapsed, clutching himself. His eyes shut tightly, pushing back memories that threatened the stability of his mind, heaving against the obsession that had driven him so far.

He clamped down on his core, ceasing to extrude chi. He let the threads he'd gathered disperse and the fade. When it was done, he collapsed, senseless and defenseless, in a circle of glimmering light beside the dead body of the cloud leopard and a paper that had been shredded in the meantime.

Lips thinned, Shan Lin carefully stole his way over to the Elder. Bending, he brushed a hand across Zhao Wan's face, seeing the youth on the boy's face. Perhaps the boy had seen much, done much in his journey to becoming an Elder that the old man did not understand. But here, lying defenseless, the hurt youth that had chosen this path of loneliness and severance was all too evident.

"What drives you, boy?" Shan Lin asked the still figure. "What did the heavens do to you?"

No surprise that there was no answer.

***

Zhao Wan woke with a start, jerking upright. He collapsed sideways, pain echoing through his body from the injuries he had sustained. The pain was worse than any simple physical injury, for he had added to the damage he had done to himself while severing the karmic string between him and Shan Lin. He knew, without a doubt, that his cultivation base, his techniques were damaged. Not irrevocably, but weakened for sure.

"You're awake." Shan Lin came over with a cup, offering it to him. "Drink. And take it easy."

Zhao Wan took the cup and drank deeply. He even took the refill without a word, sipping more gradually now.

"You gave me a scare there, boy." Shan Lin glared at Zhao Wan. "When you had those threads, those karmic strings out, you tore at them. Do you remember that?"

Zhao Wan nodded.

"Why did you do it? You had to know it was dangerous. Foolish even. I sensed what happened when you cut the string when we sparred." Shan Lin touched his chest then, as if remembering the attack. "I sensed you afterward. The way your aura had shredded."

Zhao Wan winced. He had not realized the other had sensed the damage. Had not realized that the pain he had caused himself was that visible, that clear. It had never been a problem in the Energy Storage stage. Then again, he had never dealt with that many Core Formation cultivators before. And certainly not used his technique on them.

"So, why do it?" Shan Lin asked again.

The other cultivator stayed silent, draining the last of the cup. He put his hand out for more water and watched as it was filled, pushing himself all the way to a sitting position.

"You owe me. I stopped you. You *owe me*."

Zhao Wan winced, feeling the way those words resonated. He felt the string thrum with those words, a thickened cord of karma between the pair. In his stupidity, in his pain and need, he had created a scenario that put him more in debt to the other. He could not cut the thread, could not break it. Not the way he was right now.

But perhaps he could make it a little thinner.

"I… need to be free. I can't stay here. Not now, not ever," Zhao Wan said, his voice soft at first but growing harder as he spoke. "Can you not understand? We're bound in a cycle of pain and regret, of karma and debt and repayment. Again and again, we're reborn and forced to play out the same game, while those above us laugh. They could fix it. Guide us, teach us, bring us to the next level. Instead, they bind us to this world, to run it over and over again."

"If you hate the Middle Kingdom so much, why not join the Buddhists? Stay in a temple, achieve nirvana, and escape?"

"Because they escape. It's running away. Just like the rest of those fools who travel to mountains to be a hermit," Zhao Wan said aggressively, his true feelings bursting forth from him. "I won't run. But I won't dance to their tune, not anymore."

"Not anymore?" Shan Lin said.

Zhao Wan clamped his teeth shut, refusing to answer. He might owe a debt, but there were some answers, some truths that transcended that kind of obligation. After a time, as he slowly cycle-breathed so that the pain was sent to the background, Zhao Wan stood. He tied the sword sheath to his side before rolling up the bedroll and storing it in his ring.

"You're going?" Shan Lin asked.

Dryly, Zhao Wan asked, "Did you think I did all that for my amusement? I have a lead now."

"How…?"

"I found the thread tying me to whatever hurt Elder Tung. Now, I'll follow it and finish this."

"That simple?"

"Of course." The younger cultivator hesitated, glancing at the cemetery and village below. He stared at the evening sun, then eventually shook his head. He knew better than to ask. Still, a part of him wanted to do so. "Watch yourself. Though I found a single thread, more could lead from there."

Shan Lin laughed, thumping his chest. "It's fine, young cultivator. I won't die before you pay your debt."

Snorting, Zhao Wan inclined his head in thanks. Then, turning from the man, he focused on the burning energy, that line of inquiry he had paid for in blood and soul, and followed it. Slower than usual, but he was, if anything, stubborn.

Chapter 12

Alone again. Or for the first time in a while, since the journey to the Forgotten Vale Sect had been replete with unwanted company. From the carriage master to the boatman to the random travelers on the road, Zhao Wan had been burdened with the presence of others for weeks now. Perhaps that explained the loss of control, his impatience when he'd struck out at the threads. His failure.

Discussing long-held motivations that he rarely spoke of and even more rarely deigned to acknowledge, to himself or others, smarted. What kind of cultivator grew their cultivation base not from some high-minded ideal or greedy desire for immortality but something as base as resentment?

Resentment of the very act of existence, of being tied to the dictates and debts of past lives that he neither remembered nor had chosen. A karmic wheel that ground him down, that took the lives of his family in a bout of illness and saw the love of his youth kill herself as her body rotted from within, an unspeakable, unhealable malady taking her voice, her looks, and her physical control, inch by inch?

What right did these impersonal, all-knowing wheels of karmic debt have to judge anyone? The beggar who stole for his family was as guilty as the merchant who stole for pleasure? Pains and indignities of the body and soul, decreed before birth, driving another to speak, to act in pain and shame. To curse another out, to strike at servants when the humiliation grew too great.

Was that right? Was that fair? How were you meant to resolve such failures, but with a saintly grace that even the Buddha might not achieve?

No. He would not dance to that tune. He would tear himself free. And if the very idea of such a dao, of unlimited freedom even from the heavens was borderline heretical, then so be it.

Though he would never have, should never have, spoken the words so clearly to another.

Zhao Wan knew he had enemies, individuals who were jealous of his rise and his status. Elders in other sects who sought to pull down the Verdant Green Waters, to increase their own standing. As though dragging others lower made them taller, instead of dragging everyone else into the muck.

A foolish thing, one would think, when the entire point of cultivation was striding ever higher until one reached the peak and became an immortal. Yet though many spoke of reaching such an end, Zhao Wan no longer believed that most cultivators held such ambitions.

Of course, the majority of Body Cleansing cultivators—the mortals that made up the masses—were lacking in desire. They sought to feed their family, work their farms, and love their partners. Such grinding lives of mediocrity were theirs to choose, but those who joined the sects should have been cut from a different cloth.

Most weren't.

Most only sought to rise to a position of power, to use cultivation as a tool to grow their strength or their family's strength. There was no deeper goal, no search for a dao that would carry them forth. It was why such a stark divide stood between the peak of Energy Storage and Core Formation. For the courage and the ambition to step across the threshold was lacking in many, the danger of demise during the transition significant.

Yet even among the Core Formation cultivators, the Elders of his Sect and the sects of the Shen kingdom, individuals who had found a dao that should carry them further... they were lacking. Many grew frustrated by the obscurity of their dao, others content in the strength and power of their new existence. Some grew disillusioned when constant growth of the past became a grind.

Thus, the politics began. The petty jealousies and the desire for control and status that they no longer had, as prodigies of the past, now mere mortals of the present.

Never mind the meddlers. The tricksters. The politicians whose very dao required them to indulge in such frustrating practices, binding others into their snares.

Every step took Zhao Wan deeper into the forest, away from the main roads—hah! They were barely dirt tracks in these outskirts—that had linked the village to others before. Out here, on the edge of what civilization would be, there were but rolling hills and tall bamboo forests, land that had yet to be tamed into farmland for the people.

He stalked through the forest, following the thread he had paid a blood price for. Every step sent animals scurrying and birds and insects into deep, terrified silence. Unintentionally, he leaked his blood lust, his anger and disappointment with the mundane world into the air around him, his spiritual sense and aura suffocating and warning away the creatures of the forest.

It was not a wise action.

He was not in the cultivated, often walked forests of his Sect or near major cities. Out here, Spirit Beasts centuries-old held sway, their dominion unchallenged by even the strongest cultivator. Rumors abounded of dragons and pixiu who resided in such lands, wolves and bears who solidified their domains through blood and death.

The challenge he leaked through his aura would be met at some point. He knew it, he understood it. It was why gatherers and other explorers of the deep wilds learned to contain and hide their presence, traversing such lands like thieves in the night to steal the bounty of nature.

Spirit herbs centuries old, lying untouched and undesired by Demonic and Spirit Beasts who had no need for that particular herb. Trees whose sap glistened with their contained wisdom and chi. The occasional prey animal, carefully tended and grown strong, slain for their beast cores.

Intelligent, smart, and careful such individual cultivators must be.

Not angry, hurt, and looking to lash out like the wandering sword cultivator, he whose pain stood raw upon his skin and soul, throbbing with the exposure of old wounds.

***

Hours later, Zhao Wan managed to calm his anger. He no longer stalked through the forest with a glare on his face and death in his heart. He even forcibly suppressed his aura, bringing the leaked killing intent down from multiple li to only tens of feet around him.

As he managed to find peace, he also found himself focusing upon the world. Though the strings of fate bound everything, even the mountains and trees, the ponds and the clouds, it did not mean that they were at fault. A stone kicked onto a roadway might cause an accident with a wagon a day later, but the stone had no choice. It was an innocent actor in the string of fate and karma, played out by uncaring immortals.

From that understanding, Cheng Zhao Wan could find beauty in the world around him. The untouched land of the forest, the sun slipping through the leaves, the brush of wind on his skin. He breathed deeply, the dense foliage offering a unique, natural scent that mixed with the fragrance of wildflowers and new rain.

A small twinge in his dantian, the thread leading away shifting. Zhao Wan cocked his head as he changed direction as well. Over the past few hours, minute alterations had occurred, lending credence to the idea that the cause of Elder Tung's sickness was organic and alive.

A demonic beast prowling its newly captured domain? A group of mortal bandits who had stumbled upon forgotten ruins and unearthed a cursed sword? A demon perhaps, freed from the ruins? Certainly, those options were more likely now than ever.

It mattered not. Zhao Wan would find the cause, deal with it as he had promised the Patriarch, and free himself from the debt owed to Elder Tung. That the man had demanded Zhao Wan find the traitor in his own sect mattered not, if he was delirious. Only the removal of the thread.

When that was done, Zhao Wan would return to his sect, his abode, and his contemplation of the karmic threads that bound him. And damn that fool for saving his life.

Chapter 13

Two days of traveling through the deep woods saw Zhao Wan fight twice as many battles with creatures that thought him prey. The most annoying were a horde of sapient monkeys that worked together under the aegis of a monkey king, pelting him with nuts and fruit and congealed feces from afar. It had taken him slaying a score of the horde, including three of the monkey king's guardians, before the group had retreated, leaving him alone.

The monkeys were the most annoying, but the most dangerous was a creature that sneaked up on Zhao Wan in the middle of the night, bypassing the security talismans utilized by the swordsman before it struck. Only it's misestimation of the kind of defense that Zhao Wan's robes offered had saved the cultivator, leaving him with a deep wound in his torso and a lopped off, semi-translucent limb as his survival prize.

Bandaging himself and applying high grade healing pills allowed Zhao Wan to continue his journey, though more sedately and carefully. The deep wilds were not a place for the casual cultivator, and the wound was a reminder to Zhao Wan that he had significantly more work to do. After all, he had only layered his core a single time, when the minimum number required for ascension was seven—and more often, nine to thirteen layers were recommended, depending on the cultivation method used.

Two days of travel, and in the evening of the second, Zhao Wan finally found his target. He had missed them entirely, having walked past the encampment once before the shifting thread within his soul alerted him of his mistake. Only upon closer inspection, rotating through his spiritual and other sensory techniques, had Zhao Wan recognized the beguiling illusion formation flags in place.

Another man might have sought a less direct method of dealing with the formation and the illusion itself. Another cultivator might have parted the formation with skills and enchantments of their own. Or sat, hidden, high above to watch the encampment location until their prey left. Another individual might have chosen subtlety and care.

Zhao Wan drew his sword, imparted with it the killing and blade intent he held within his soul, and cut once, parting the illusion formation such that he could step through the wavering enchantment. He strode in through the tear in space and twisted light even as the rush of new odors informed him of what was behind the formation. A simple flickering campfire, a quartet of grey-black robed cultivators reaching for their weapons, and their captives.

The young swordsman's gaze flicked sideways, even as his spiritual senses extended to the full extent of the encampment. He took in the group of mortals huddled a distance away, shivering in the falling cold of the evening. No fire for them, bowlfuls of plain, day-old rice clutched in their hands, eaten barehanded.

As Zhao Wan walked closer to the fire, he sheathed his weapon, nodding companionably to the cultivators who gripped their weapons and stared at him fearfully. His spiritual sense caressed their auras, feeling the strength projected outward. Three of them were inconsequential, two in the middle of the Energy Storage stage, the last a pitiful Body Cleansing cultivator. The last was a threat, another Core Formation cultivator like him, his aura pressing against Zhao Wan's in retaliation as Zhao Wan's spiritual sense washed over him. Not much stronger, if at all, than Zhao Wan.

"Greetings, fellow travelers. I sensed your presence and hope to join you by your fire." Zhao Wan ignored the fact of his own intrusive, rude, and violent entry as he crossed the short distance to stand before the quartet. "If you do not mind, of course."

Flabbergasted by his words and his attitude, the group stared. After a moment, the Core Formation cultivator laughed, standing as he sheathed his dao. The curved sword slipped into its place by his belt before the man offered Zhao Wan a clasped hand greeting.

"Of course, of course. You are welcome to our fire. It is dangerous to travel in such lands alone." He gestured to a nearby seat, waving his people so that an opening was made for Zhao Wan. He looked at the one moving, his throat bobbing a little as he sent the man a chi-laden, hidden message. "Tell me, who is it who asks for our company this evening?"

Zhao Wan idly noted that the seat offered to him was in the direction that the smoke blew, but he chose not to comment as he sat. "Cheng Zhao Wan, Elder of the Verdant Green Waters Sect greets you." Not that his affiliation was hard to miss, what with the black robes in green trim that he wore or the sect insignia that had been stitched into the left breast of the robes. Still, there were forms to be followed.

"Yong Hai Tian. I hail from a small sect one as prestigious as yourself would not have known," Hai Tian said. "These are my fellow sect members."

Zhao Wan noted how none of the three had been introduced. Or the fact that two of them had yet to drop their weapons. Only the third cultivator, the Body Cleansing cultivator, had set down his weapon. Now, the third placed a pot of wine on top of a bowl of water on a heated rock near the fire, before picking up a ladle to stir the stewpot. Within the stew, a bubbling meal of ginger and crushed garlic, wild foraged mushrooms and soy sauce bubbled. Chunks of rough-cut pale meat floated, breaking apart gradually.

"I am quite widely read. Most of my sect Elders are," Zhao Wan said. "And if I have not heard of it, I would take it as a kindness if you enlightened me."

Hai Tian hesitated for a moment, his eyes flicking sideways, away from Zhao Wan. After a moment, he answered. "Of course. We're the Three Fallen Log clan."

Zhao Wan did not even need to look to the side to know where the inspiration for that lie had come from. Really? Fallen log, after staring at the minor boundary created by a series of collapsed trees? Then again, they were all lying to some extent in this interaction.

The question was, who lied better?

"And your other companions?" Zhao Wan said, inclining his head in the direction of the huddled mortals. "Who are they?"

"Just fellow travelers. We graciously agreed to take care of them whilst traveling through these treacherous lands," Hai Tian said. "What brings an Elder of the Verdant Green Waters through this land? We are far from your esteemed sect."

"We are," Zhao Wan said. "I am here on a personal matter and obligation."

As he spoke, he drew a deep breath, letting the Thousand Miseries technique activate. Immediately, he was assaulted by the smell of the food, the slightly damp wood used for the fireplace, the redolent warming wine. But beneath all that, he noted another, stronger smell. One that stank of tar and deceased flesh, that made his face twist in disbelief. It came from the wine pot and the villagers, though not all of them. How many were infected, he could not tell, but it was certain that they were.

"Ah, obligations are difficult, are they not? But what a poor host I am." Hai Tian gestured to the Body Cleansing cultivator, who picked up the wine pot and a small cup, pouring the wine gracefully.

As he did so, the rotting smell intensified, forcing Zhao Wan to stop using the Thousand Miseries technique or retch.

"Please!" Hai Tian took the cup from his companion and leaned forward, over the gap between the pair, offering the wine to Zhao Wan.

Zhao Wan reached forward and pushed on the hand with the back of his, even as he answered. "No, no. How can I, a guest, drink before the host?"

Hai Tian's eyes narrowed and he disengaged, slipping his hand under Zhao Wan's by rolling his wrist. He kept the cup stable, the liquid not sloshing at all as he did so.

"Ah, but you are late to the party. We have been drinking already. This pot was set to warm just for you," Hai Tian said, shifting forward even further and bringing the drink closer to Zhao Wan.

Rather than answer, the young cultivator turned his hand over a little, striking with his fingers on the inside of Hai Tian's forearm. He hit the pressure point with subtle pressure, sending only a touch of his chi and blade intent within. Hai Tian's hand spasmed open, the cup dropping.

Only to be caught by Zhao Wan with his other hand. He twisted the cup as it was caught, tossing the liquid into the fire and in the direction of the two Energy Storage cultivators. The moment the liquid struck the fire, the merry orange glow became a sickly green and a noxious cloud rolled in the direction of the toss.

The pair of cultivators scrambled backward, one going so far as to hold a hand up to his face. The second stood, the guan dao he had been holding by his side leveled at the swordsman.

"Oh my. How clumsy of us. Spilling your wine into the fire," Zhao Wan said, sitting back as he dropped the cup onto the ground where it shattered. "And breaking the cup."

"You..." Hai Tian hissed, having pulled his hand back and cradling it a little as he rubbed at the pressure point. "Are we done with the pretense then?"

"It seems so." Zhao Wan turned his gaze on the guan dao wielder as he moved to strike at him, freezing his opponent in his tracks as he sharpened his killing intent. The other man started sweating, unable to move. "But we can still speak, can we not?"

"What is there to speak of?" Hai Tian said curiously. The Core Formation cultivator smoothed down his grey-black robes, ran a hand through his hair, and adjusted the pin holding the mid-shoulder-length hair back as he spoke.

Not once did the other cultivators even look at the huddled mortals, many of whom had shrunk even farther back to the edges of the formation, food clutched tightly, eyes wide with fear. Silent as an unspoiled cemetery awaiting its next resident.

"Many things." Zhao Wan smiled grimly. "After all, there is much we can tell one another. The dead speak no secrets, for they forget all sins before their rebirth, though they bear many grudges."

"Are you threatening us then?" Hai Tian said, smirking now. "You might not have noticed, but we outnumber you."

"Just stating a truth." Zhao Wan's hands turned palm up on his legs. "One party will not see the dawn. We might as well settle any curiosities beforehand."

Hai Tian stared at the young Elder before he broke into a laugh. He slapped his leg as he laughed, stopping and starting again and again until he calmed down. "Oh, you are a brave and audacious one. If you were not so upright, you might even be a good recruit."

"Upright?"

"I saw your eyes, the look of disgust when you spotted the mortals. As though they and their lives matter at all to those of us who sit above them," Hai Tian said, his voice shifting as he spoke. Gone were the initial tones of polite interest, and now came the natural arrogance of one who had seen few setbacks through his fortunate life.

"What do you intend with them?" Zhao Wan said, his gaze flicking toward the huddled mortals.

"Myself?" Hai Tian snorted. "Nothing. I am but a delivery person. I bring them to be dealt with by others."

"The village," Zhao Wan said.

"Ah, I see you came from there." Hai Tian nodded, as Zhao Wan confirmed a suspicion. "Yes. The village. The conditions in the ruin are good, the feng shui strong for our purposes."

"And those are?"

"Not for me to say," Hai Tian said. "But tell me, how did you find us? A talisman? An enchantment? How did you pierce my formation?"

Zhao Wan considered not answering. But the exchange of information between the two was useful for him. It was why he had chosen to speak rather than kill them. If he chose not to answer, the conversation would likely be over. Then, it would be time for the killing.

And as he had said, dead men spoke little.

"A ritual technique. One unique to myself," Zhao Wan said, eyeing the man. When it seemed what he said was insufficient, he continued. "It combined foretelling and karmic weighting, allowing me to ascertain the karmic path between the two of us."

"A powerful technique." Hai Tian let his gaze roam over Zhao Wan. The younger cultivator knew what he might see—the slight hunch in his posture from the wound in his stomach, the frayed aura at the edges where he had injured himself while using the technique, the bags under his eyes, when ill rest had left him with exhaustion in his bones. "But one not without cost."

"All things have a cost. As it seems, the poison that you have wielded," Zhao Wan threw out, curious to see their reactions.

"It's not much cost at all," Hai Tian said. "A few mortals, some animals. Some time. But if we perfect it…" A bright smile then. "But then, people like you would stop us, no? Even if the research we do might benefit all cultivators, you feel the mortals must be protected. As though they matter. As though they have not chosen their fates. The lives they live, it's a mess. Pitiful. Not that you'd know either, would you? You're no peasant."

"No, I'm not." Zhao Wan smiled a little grimly. "But just because I do not hail from their stock does not mean I care for the waste of their lives, their chances at redeeming their karmic debts."

"Why bother?" Hai Tian said. "Why care for these ants? They are as numerous as the insects, prone to repopulating themselves just as much."

Zhao Wan fell silent. Hai Tian shifted a little, impatient as the silence stretched. The other cultivators shifted in their seats, some moving to flank the quiet young cultivator, who made no motion to stop them.

"I am no peasant. My parents were scholar-bureaucrats. Once upon a time, I was to become a scholar too. I trained, I studied, then…" Zhao Wan shook his head as he recollected the disease that had spread through their city, that saw hundreds driven to death as mortals huddled in their homes in fear. It was freeing, funnily enough, to speak with a cultivator who would never speak again of what he was about to say. "Then the wheel turned, and they died. And I was set upon the path of cultivation.

"And because of that, I can see the flows of karma. I can see the threads that wrap around you, from them, from those you have caused the deaths of. The burden you've placed upon your soul that must be repaid. In this life or the next."

"My soul? My debt?" Hai Tian laughed derisively. "A demon owes nothing to mortals. Our job is to be the woe to their existence. It is what we do."

"Is that what you think you are? A demon?" Zhao Wan cocked his head to the side.

"It is not what I think, it is what I am. What I will be," Hai Tian said, lips curling up.

"Ah…" Zhao Wan let out another long breath. He closed his eyes for a moment, then opened them. "Then, I guess, that answers my questions."

"Well, I have another…" Hai Tian said.

But in the middle of his words, he acted. A hand swept up the pot and threw it at Zhao Wan, even as he stood and dropped his hand—not to his sword but between the folds of his robes. Meanwhile, the other cultivators acted as well, a moment behind their leader. Weapons swung, each aimed for the still-seated cultivator.

Chapter 14

Poisoned wine flew through the air toward Zhao Wan, spilling out of the warm clay pot it had been contained within. As it crossed the fire, the flames turned sickly green once more as the poison diffused through the air. Rather than risk the poison breaching his aura barrier, Zhao Wan rolled backward.

No surprise his opponents had expected it. The guan dao wielder swung his polearm in a diagonal cut from the shoulder down to his hip, intent on bisecting the dodging cultivator. At the same time, an Energy Storage cultivator chose to cut with his dao, extending his weapon with his chi such that it encompassed the space Zhao Wan was meant to dodge into.

Finally, the third enemy cultivator thrust forward with his jian, extending the blade with his chi too. A coordinated attack, one that had been planned while Zhao Wan had been speaking. There were no gaps in it, no way for him to move without being struck.

So he did not.

Zhao Wan strengthened his aura, raising his left hand as he blocked the cut from the dao. As he did so, he turned his body such that he dodged under the diagonal attack that had meant to bisect him. As for the jian, he kicked the rock he had worked under his foot as he rolled, sending the projectile into his opponent's chin.

The rock struck its target, the cultivator's jaw shattering under the attack. He stumbled, his forward momentum robbed, and fell sideways into the poisonous cloud. Immediately, his face turned green, suffusing with sickness as the poison took effect. Clawing at his throat and eyes, the dying man thrashed, his clothing and parts of his hair catching alight as well.

Hai Tian snarled at the thrashing body, kicking it to send the man flying and clearing the way to Zhao Wan. In the meantime, having blocked and then caught the dao with his bare hand, his blade intent overwhelming his opponent's attack, Zhao Wan now ripped the weapon away by using the momentum of his roll before he threw it at the polearm wielder. On his knees, he rose up and spun, finishing the initial moments of the fight with a simple spinning kick that sent the former dao wielder flying away.

A glance to the side showed the polearm wielder collapsed over the embedded sword in his chest, and Zhao Wan smirked at Hai Tian.

"You were speaking of being outnumbered?" As he spoke, the swordsman flicked down Hai Tian's body, noting the still sheathed dao.

Instead, Hai Tian held something smaller and less conspicuous.

A brush.

"An interesting choice of a weapon," Zhao Wan said. "I thought I was the former scholar."

Hai Tian chose not to answer, instead flicking forward the hand he held down by his side. From it sprang talismans, dozens of yellow slips of paper with pre-inscribed enchantments on them. They flew toward Zhao Wan, tendrils of chi connecting the talismans to his opponent.

Wary of the potential tricks the man might play, Zhao Wan backed off. Trickster for sure, carrying a dao but specializing in formations. Zhao Wan kicked at the earth, sending a spray of dirt and stone at the talismans as he retreated. The stones and dirt he'd sprayed moved at a speed that should have torn the plain paper apart, but they did not, the attack only managing to divert a few talismans. However, a handful of the talismans struck and exploded, small flames consuming the inscribed yellow paper and the area around them. A couple other talismans were caught in those flames, but that left dozens of the yellow papers still flying toward Zhao Wan.

"Formation masters…" he growled, finally choosing to draw his sword.

Zhao Wan fell into the defensive stance from the first form of the Sundering Blade, Warding pests after an Inheritance. The form was made of fast, quick cuts that allowed him to weave a defensive net against numerous fast-moving objects like the "good" intentions of strangers.

Under the blade intent of his weapon, the unusually hardy talismans came apart, their separated sides falling to the ground. The controlling power of the enchantments broken, the talismans became no more than plain paper.

In the meantime, Hai Tian had used the time bought for him to scribble upon a series of blank paper talismans floating in the air before him. His brush flowed from strip of paper to strip of paper, new words formed with each passing of his brush. The enchanted brush required no ink, forming it from the very air as it embedded chi instructions into the newly formed talismans.

Talisman creation was a powerful enchanting form, though it often required significant care and precision. It was particularly useful for cultivators who had smaller dantians and cores, allowing them to borrow energy from the environment to empower the talismans and release them later.

Already, Zhao Wan felt the churn of environmental chi as the talismans drew energy toward themselves, robbing the surroundings of energy. They fluttered a little in the cyclone that grew, water and wind chi pulled toward them. Tendrils of flame rose from the fire to embed themselves amidst the grouping even as shards of earth broke free, clumps of metal rising before they reached the talismans and fell once again.

The initial onslaught of prepared magical inscriptions dealt with, Zhao Wan turned his attention to his opponent. He swung his blade once and then again, cutting an x of energy that was meant to bisect the man, pouring blade energy and killing intent into the attack.

Smirking behind his wall of talismans, Hai Tian dabbed at four of the newly made inscriptions. They flew forward, forming a small rectangle before stolen earth chi exploded forth.

A dull brown shield of earth energy formed in the air moments before Zhao Wan's attack struck, shattering both.

In the time between, four more slips of paper had flown from Hai Tian's sleeve to take the empty spaces created by the movement of the initial four. Already, his brush was marking them, even as other talismans, having drawn their fill from the environmental chi, were pulled away to float above Hai Tian's shoulders and new blank slips of paper took their places.

"An interesting tactic, talisman master. Most would have written their talismans beforehand," Zhao Wan said. He cut again, twice more in quick succession, watching as his attacks broke against new shields. Each time, four more talismans took their place. After the second attack, a glyphed, glowing silver shield of metallic chi formed.

"Formation master. The talismans are but a tool." Hai Tian made a small gesture, eight talismans flying out from behind him to strike the formation flags.

Immediately, Zhao Wan noticed the change in the environment as the former illusion formation transformed. No longer a deceptive formation meant to hide them. Now, it was a beguiling formation. In the time that Zhao Wan had looked away, his opponent had moved, and now there were three figures with just as many talismans floating in front of him. Shields of water, metal, and earth floated before each of those figures.

Even with his spiritual sense fully extended, Zhao Wan could not tell the difference between the three. They looked, they moved like one another. Zhao Wan sharpened his killing intent, wielding it as a weapon, but watched all three flinch in unison.

"Mirrored images of one another, eh?" Zhao Wan muttered. Not as powerful a technique as independently moving figures, but useful for hiding one's intentions. Even now, the figures were creating new talismans.

The longer this battle lasted, the more dangerous it would grow.

Zhao Wan was not ignorant of the talismans that had slipped away during the fight and were taking position in the corners of a pentagram around him. There weren't enough of them yet, for there were spots still empty. When the hastily constructed formation was finished, however, the battle would likely take another turn.

And while Zhao Wan might have enjoyed that, they weren't alone in the clearing. So far, the huddled group of mortals had been left untouched by the battle. When the formation activated, Zhao Wan could not promise that fortunate events would continue.

So he acted.

First, he cut sideways, a diagonal strike that stretched from one side of his body to the other. An uncommonly used technique, Bisecting the

Will. Still from the first form of the Sundered Blade, but combined with his chi and blade intent, the arc of energy struck at all three shields at once. They flared brightly, blocking the view of himself.

Next came A Storm of Missives, a series of cuts thrown from elbow and shoulder. Zhao Wan had to admit, if one cornered him, that the first form took little from the strength of the jian, other than its dexterity. It leaned heavily into cuts, into blade attacks and aggressive forms rather than the more delicate subtlety in the center of the weapon's heart.

Then again, the entire form had been formed around a period of great personal turmoil. When he had not sought subtlety in the expression of his feelings, having been aggrieved and injured in the extreme. Instead, he'd sought to lash out again and again at his opponents.

Now, he chose to do so again.

Strikes of blade intent shattered against the shields, wasted upon at least two of those shields. It mattered not, for they all cracked, only to be replaced by other shields of wood and water. No fire shields, Zhao Wan noted, even as he poured more energy into the attack.

Talismans burned up, falling to the ground one after the other. Behind the shields, more talismans drew upon the churning chi released into the clearing, filled themselves to bursting and flying through the sky to take position. The talismans bobbed like overly large fireflies in the night. Energy rotated through them as the formation neared completion.

No more time to delay.

Zhao Wan finished the form, the air humming with power and the hiss of flying blade projections. In the storm of energy and light, Zhao Wan crouched low and exhaled before he exploded forward.

He rocketed forward in a passing lunge that carried him across the clearing. Even as the latest shield broke under the onslaught of his earlier attacks, Zhao Wan passed through the newly forming shield of water and the talisman wall before him, his skin warming under the onslaught of energy that brushed against his aura.

His sword glowed with blade energy, his entire body wreathed as his aura extended outward as a form of defense as talismans, disrupted from their positioning, exploded in a scintillating fury of light and sound, elemental energy washing over him. Sword held before him, Zhao Wan pierced the surprised figure behind the talisman wall with ease. He felt his blade sink through the chest, entering halfway through the body before their momentum carried them both backward, his form completed.

The Final Stroke.

High above, the glowing talismans exploded as the fiery energy within went out of control as Hai Tian's concentration failed him. Pinned on the jian, he struggled weakly, pulling some of the remaining talismans toward him to strike back.

Before the talismans could arrive, the pair impacted the edge of the beguilement formation and a tree outside the formation itself. Head slamming into the hard wood, his body wracked with pain, Hai Tian lost control of his last attack as Zhao Wan pulsed his sword aura, sending tiny blades arcing from the jian into the man's body.

"How? How did you know it was me?" Hai Tian asked, his other hand clutching at the blade embedded in his chest, blood dribbling from his lips to stain the earth.

"The karmic threads followed you still," Zhao Wan replied.

Then he twisted with his hips, ripping the sword from the man's body. Fingers flew through the air, even as heart blood pulsed, filling the atmosphere with a fine spray of blood.

Hai Tian coughed, once and then again, before he slumped down the trunk to the ground, lifeless.

Chapter 15

Zhao Wan regarded the still body for a moment before bending down and relieving it of the dagger and dao by its side, then he rolled up the sleeves to locate the talisman papers hidden within. He then stored the enchanted brush, along with the rest of his loot, in his storage ring and, after waving his hand over the body to ascertain chi flow, removed the storage ring hung from a string around the neck of the corpse's body.

Certain that his most dangerous opponent had been dealt with, he stood and regarded the surroundings. He ignored the two bodies of those he had slain himself, moving to the third cultivator. He had purposely struck him with his foot, hoping to have a prisoner to question further.

However, his hopes were not to bear fruit.

Somewhere during the fight, a single talisman had fallen onto the body and wrapped itself around the man's face, constricting his breathing and silently suffocating the unconscious figure to death. It seemed that even through the battle, Hai Tian had planned for defeat.

Zhao Wan could not help but silently acknowledge Hai Tian's ability and conviction. If not his morals. Even he, who sought to distance himself from the turning of the wheel and humanity by virtue of his choices, would not have taken such amoral action.

A whimper echoed through the clearing as though in counterpoint to his thoughts. Remembering the mortals, Zhao Wan walked over to the crowd of villagers huddled in the corner of the clearing. The group had shrunk from the fight, laying themselves flat or curled up in balls, and even so, many bore scorch marks from the flaring energies at the end. As he neared, they shrank away, causing his lips to tighten.

Gratitude, such a fleeting emotion.

"Which ones of you are poisoned?" Zhao Wan asked sternly. When there was no immediate answer, he repeated the question more forcefully.

"You can't have her!" a woman called from within the group.

"I want nothing of her. I seek to understand the poison itself," Zhao Wan said. "Show me the poisoned ones." He considered for a second, then added, "Perhaps there might be an antidote with the corpses."

His words garnered the response he was looking for, as a pair of individuals pushed away from the crowd. One was an older man clutching his arm. Now that he was free from the crowd, it was simple to note the cut that ran horizontally along his left arm, the spreading darkness and the overpowering smell of rot that rose from it. Before he could take more than a step, Zhao Wan's hand shot out to grip the man's other shoulder, pulling him to a halt.

The other scrambling villager, an older woman with greying hair, he let go. She had no smell of rot on her. In the short time when the crowd had opened to release the pair, Zhao Wan had spotted his true second target. A girl, no older than ten perhaps, lay on the ground, unconscious. She had the very same injury, but on the other arm.

"Why did you not at least wrap the injury?" Zhao Wan asked the man curiously. At the same time, his spiritual senses roamed over the man, judging his aura and checking on his health as best he could. Mild fever, though his eyes were clear. The wound itself had scabbed over, though dark, putrid liquid seeped from the edges of the wound and cracked scab. At least a day or two then, since the initial infection.

"They would not let us," said one of the others in the crowd, their voice muffled.

The injured man had shrunk in on himself, refusing to meet Zhao Wan's eyes or speak to him. The cultivator frowned a little, but turned the victim slightly with his hand so that he could inspect the wound more closely. Releasing the man's arm, Zhao Wan raised the injured arm with his fingertips, peering at it more closely even as he activated the Thousand Miseries.

Once more, his senses were assaulted by the necrotic stink of the poison acting upon the mortal. Zhao Wan removed his dagger and, while holding the man's hand steady, moved it toward the wound. The older man held still, compliant in a beaten, broken manner.

Not so the speaker from the huddle who stood up unsteadily. His face was gaunt, haggard with lack of food and sleep, but there was still fire in his eyes. "What are you doing?"

"Inspecting the wound. I intend no harm, but I must understand this poison." Zhao Wan paused, then added, "And the people who inflicted it. Tell me, where did they acquire you?

How long have they held you? What do you know of their plans?"

"You promise?"

"I do. Now answer me."

"I… we've been walking for weeks now. We were all from the same village. There were dozens of us when we started. They came and took us all, marched us into the forest." The man's voice grew pained, his eyes haunted. "So many died. From the beasts, from the cultivators when they tried to run. They laughed when they did it, punished those who stayed and those who helped. Or just watched as another tried to run.

"They started experimenting on us the day after. Doing… that."

Zhao Wan listened, cataloguing the words as he gently sliced a scab open. He pressed on the newly revealed skin, watched as gangrenous skin erupted with yellow-and-green pus and black liquid. The smell grew even stronger and the man he held whimpered, tugging futilely at his hand. He might as well have tried to shift a mountain. Even the villager who had dared speak shrank away, holding a hand to his nose.

It was a memorable smell, one that Zhao Wan had noted emanating from Elder Tung. Slightly different—a little fresher, a little more brackish. He pressed on the wound with his knife, allowing the fluid to gather above his blade before releasing the arm to view the poison.

Then, turning from the pair, Zhao Wan walked over to the fire and held the dagger to the flame. He watched the poison change color, watched the flame above the poison change to that same noxious green flame from before.

"How did they introduce the poison?" Zhao Wan asked.

"The cut, Honored Benefactor." Now the brave villager was being polite, almost sycophantic.

"Only the cut?"

Silence, then slowly, "They did feed it to some, in the beginning. But they said it was not strong enough. Not yet. Some of those they fed it to, they survived."

"Interesting."

Finally, the older woman returned, clutching bottles in her hands. She offered them to Zhao Wan. "Honored Cultivator. Please. I do not know…"

"You should not touch them with your bare hands." Pulling on his chi, Zhao Wan floated the bottles from her to the ground, pulling out a silk cloth from his ring before depositing the bottles on them.

The woman was holding her hands before her dumbly, looking around before she squatted and rubbed them on the dirt. "My niece. Please…"

"I heard you. But I am no physician." Using the tip of his blade, now cleaned of the poison by the flame and plunged into the dirt a few times, Zhao Wan lifted the leather labels tied around each pill bottle. He frowned and read the notation offered on each pill bottle, the names on the front. "Is this all?"

"Yes, Honored Cultivator. All that I could see. But the magic rings you use…" She ducked her head. "I don't know…"

"Ah." Zhao Wan let out an annoyed huff before standing. Pointing at the bottles, he continued. "Don't touch those three with the red caps. The rest are nothing more than normal medicines. Those of you who can read might want to use them. Though I would not put it above these cultivators to trap them as well."

Then, moving to the other bodies, he searched for storage rings. He found only one, on the poisoner's hand. A small thing that had been placed around his smallest finger, a thin band of white jade that was easy to overlook.

Pulling the jade band off the body, he frowned at the corpses. The night was still young and having them in the clearing would likely be an issue. His storage ring was not large enough to store four bodies, and a quick check indicated that the two new rings were not exceptional. So storing the corpses that way was impossible.

Not that he necessarily wanted to infect his ring with the bodies. If they used poison…

"You!" He pointed at the villager who had spoken to him. When he startled and looked at Zhao Wan, he gestured to the bodies. "Take the bodies outside the formation. Make sure to go a good distance, then leave them."

"But… out there…"

"Nothing is nearby," Zhao Wan said curtly. He flexed his aura, pressuring the few smaller, weaker creatures around that might be a bother for the plain mortals. "But that might not last. So work fast." He paused, looking over the bodies. "You might want to search them for other items. Money, jewelry. You will need it to grow your village."

"You'd leave that to us, Honored Benefactor?" the man said.

"They are not mine. And their owners are dead."

Still, the villager hesitated until Zhao Wan glared. Then the man gestured at a few of the other villagers, some of whom had begun to relax and move apart. Chivied into motion, they reached for the first body and scoured it for valuables, some even beginning an argument about if they should strip the body entirely. After all, there was not *that* much blood on the pants.

Zhao Wan disregarded them, instead pouring his senses into the storage rings he had acquired. The formation master's was typical in its contents. A larger-than-normal quantity of clothing, lots of writing implements, paper, and some books. After extracting the books, Zhao Wan flipped through them, making the books disappear back into the ring as he ascertained their contents.

Nothing unusual. A few cultivation techniques—one for a visual sense, another for movement, a third for making one's hair more lustrous. Notes on the cultivation method the man had used, though not the actual manual. More works on formation creation, from dry theoretical basics that even Zhao Wan recognized to more esoteric discussions on the proper placement of formation flags as dictated by the movement of birds or clouds. Then, of course, were the personal notes on all of it, detailed formation manuals with notations added to suit the formation master's predilections, and finally, personal reading.

Boring and predictable. As were the stack of formation flags, some wrapped around banners or formation discs or supplied with additional talismans. Perhaps the most surprising aspect was the sheer volume, for each formation flag and type were an expense. The quantity packed into the storage ring was significant, an indicator of resources and backing for the man he had killed.

Beyond that, nothing. No missives, no further details about what the man was going to do.

Lips pursed, Zhao Wan turned to the next ring. The white jade ring had the smallest storage amount, barely larger than the space for a chest. Within, he sensed a variety of bottles, a couple of daggers, and a wrapped bundle along with the usual myriad changes of clothing. In one corner of the storage ring, a small bag was located. Dirty, disheveled, and lumpy.

Out of curiosity, Zhao Wan conjured the bag. Catching it as it was pulled into his hand, he noted the crusty exterior, the dirt and rough texture of the hemp contents. Then, a moment later, the smell from the bag struck him. Slightly rotten, the smell of rotting flesh. The feel of the bag itself was strange, shifting like a series of beans were within.

Tugging open the string wrapped around the bag, he turned it over and stared at what fell into his waiting hand. His face scrunched up in disgust and only impeccable self-control stopped him from throwing aside the white, discolored, slightly rotting contents.

"He pulled them from every single one of our people when they died. Only the right canine though…" the aunt who had come to stand near Zhao Wan impatiently said. "He… he said they were his trophies."

"I… see." Pouring the contents back into the bag, Zhao Wan considered what to do with them. When he looked at the woman, hoping she had an answer, she was shaking her head furiously.

"Keep it. Those… if you can use it against them. Keep it."

Zhao Wan nodded, putting the bag away in the ring. He returned to where the medicines had been, bottles having disappeared and been passed around, leaving only a few empty bottles behind. He swept those aside before replacing them with the poisoner's ring's contents. Behind him, the woman crouched low, though she had learned her lesson and chose not to touch anything. Still, she looked impatient as Zhao Wan used his knife to shift them around until he had a view of each of the bottles.

The writing on the bottles was barely legible, a heinous crime of calligraphy compared to the elegant writings of the formation master or even the other, common pill bottles. Zhao Wan could not help but shake his head internally as he read the labels.

"Seventeenth night, third variation. Eighteenth night, sixth variation." Zhao Wan continued to frown, flicking through each bottle, one after the other. By the time he came to the end of the bottles, he knew the truth.

So did the woman sitting by his side, so filled with hope. "Please, Honored Benefactor.

Anything you can do. Please…" The woman begged, going so far as to clutch at his leg.

For a long time, Zhao Wan hesitated. Then he bent his head a little in a bow and stood to walk over to the child. He knew he should not. So far, he had done little to tie them to him. Saving their lives was a byproduct of his own quest, and though some connections had been created, it was no more than a lightning strike could be said to be owed a debt.

Now though… now he treaded dangerous waters.

Still, he had to check on the girl's wound. See if there were any differences. Any change in the way the poison interacted with the younger girl. A part of him knew he was making excuses. That it would not, should not, matter. She was a child. The other victim an adult. But both were peasants, mortals.

When he bent down next to the girl, he was struck by a few things. The first was that, even dirtied and disheveled, even ill and exhausted, even newly awake, there was a calmness to the young girl's gaze. A wisdom that was unusual, even amongst the elderly.

"May I see your injury?" Zhao Wan said, his voice softening a little.

The girl nodded mutely, offering him her arm. He took those small fingers in his, pushing back the robe with his other hand gently, even as he noted that other surprise.

She was no plain Body Cleansing cultivator, stuck at the first or second grade like so many. At her age, she should have just broken through to the first level, but here she was, having fully cleansed a third meridian and working on a fourth. It explained some of the flawless skin, the clarity in her eyes, and the healthier flush of her cheeks.

But…

Not everything.

Not the state of her wound either, the way it had grown pustulant too, but also…

"This is healing," Zhao Wan said, surprised.

"It is?" The aunt who had been hovering in the background pushed forward, then leaned in. Her nose wrinkled as she neared the injury, even as she peered at it. "I do not see it."

"Here. At the edges." Zhao Wan pointed with his knife tip. Beneath his hand, he felt the smallest tremble from the young girl, tension and fear coursing through her body. Yet her face showed no change. "But…"

"But?" the aunt asked again.

He did not answer her, realizing he was overstepping. If he did this, if he told her, if he helped… it would tie him down. Lock him into place, bind the child to him, the karmic thread between forming tight. He would need to cut this tie in some way. Have the child repay it at some point.

More. There was a thread here already, one he could sense from the past. It bound him to the girl, pulled her into his path in this life.

He should cut it now, before it grew too thick. Should not speak further but sever the tie.

If he did, she would die. The backlash, the poison, it would all be enough.

A young prodigy, a child who stared back at him with poise and calm that her own relative failed to have. It would be a shame to allow her to die when he could save her. And if he was to do something…

Choices. Ties. Debts.

Zhao Wan closed his eyes, feeling within himself. Trying to understand his own dao. Trying to grasp the path he had begun walking upon. He stayed there, unmoving, until a single voice brought him out of it.

The young girl, speaking softly. Gently. A single word. "Please."

His eyes flew open, and he regarded the girl.

Then she continued. "Please. Not like this."

An echo of another woman, another he had failed to save, rang through his mind. A child, a woman, interposed themselves. Karma? Fate? Something more than destiny or less, in the core of free will that was humanity's gift.

Time, place, destiny.

Choice.

Zhao Wan made a decision.

Chapter 16

"Sit up, take a meditative position. Cultivate, like you know how. I will provide you energy, you will take it and use it to heal yourself. Drive the toxin out." He hesitated, before continuing. "The chi I will send will be unaspected, but it is refined energy, drawn from my Core. If you cannot control it and the pain, your meridians will burn out. You will die in agony. Do you understand?"

"More horribly than this?" She raised her infected arm, and when Zhao Wan chose not to answer, she smiled impishly. A flicker of the child coming through. "Then, why not?"

Zhao Wan waited for her to take her position. She struggled upward, her face flushed as she sat upright, legs crossed while Zhao Wan put his hands on her back. He breathed in slowly, then out, instructing her to do the same.

"Tell me when you're ready," Zhao Wan told her.

It took half a dozen cycles, a short amount of time to calm the rushing heartbeat beneath his hands. He marveled again at the young lady's control, to be able to settle herself so quickly, even knowing what was to come. She did not rush either, even when she had slowed her breathing and heartbeat. Instead, she took the time to breathe a few more times, to cycle her breaths and energy before she told him to act.

He started gradually.

The amount of energy he poured into the young girl was but a tiny fraction of the energy within his core, the smallest amount he could control. He altered it from his own metal aspect to the general, unaspected energy that would suit the child. Then he handed it to her in a trickle.

She hissed, her back arching as the first flood poured within. Pain tore through her, her nerves on fire, the meridians straining to contain the potent energy. Even the trickle he sent through was more than she had cultivated to break through a single meridian, and the ten other clogged ones thrummed like a taut drum as their blockages repulsed the overflowing energy.

"Control. Direct it into the wound. You have healed it before. Do it again."

"I…. don't know how," she whispered.

"Then you die."

She had no answer to that. Could not, for he kept the energy pouring through her. She breathed slowly and carefully. Cycled the incoming energy to her dantian in her lower torso, then out to the wound in her arm. As the empowered chi flowed through her and into her arm, she felt the necrotic energy that had leached power from her body react.

First, it tried to take from the energy as it had done her own. It drained the incoming chi, spreading faster up her arm as it found a new source of strength. But glutton for energy that it was, the poison could only draw so much from the flood entering the wound.

Yang-aspected chi from Zhao Wan burned hot, feeding the necrotic poison, but once it was fully consumed, it destroyed the poison itself, driving the infection down the arm. At the same time, the child's natural yin chi cooled the meridians and flesh that came after, sweeping up the poison that had infiltrated her flesh.

"Oh, child… I'm so sorry." Her aunt was gripping her own hands, watching the pair and obviously uncertain of what to do, how to aid her. She looked between the girl and the cultivator, biting her lip so hard that she bled.

Zhao Wan rode the energy flow, his spiritual senses fully extended and narrowed into her body, her injury. He understood what was happening in her wound, grasped the difference then between the patients. This poison, it fed on the yang. With male victims, it could spread unchecked. Yin-infused individuals—women mostly—they naturally combatted and assimilated the poison itself.

If she had been stronger, the child might not have needed his help. Then again… if she was stronger, the poison would have had more energy to feed upon. It had been starved by the child and her yin energy, driven back to allow her to heal in parts while other portions kept growing worse.

Now though, there was nowhere to hide. The flood of core chi from him was tearing her apart as it did the poison, burning it away by sheer volume. His blade intent, his dao understanding filled that chi. The Sundering Blade was good at one thing, if nothing else, and that was separating. It cut, and cut again, at the poison, at the flesh that was diseased and rotting, at the wound in her arm.

He heard her cry then, a whining noise that did not stop her control of energy, the guiding will of the chi he poured into her as she directed it into her arm. Even as tears fell from her eyes, even as her breathing hitched and her body glowed from the overabundance of energy, she never lost control.

"Clean the wound," Zhao Wan remarked. He had to repeat it again, to draw the attention of the aunt before she ripped apart her own robes and wiped at the cut.

Each swipe pulled skin free, black and yellow liquid spilling out, necrotic tissue slipping free of the wound. After a few swipes, she switched the cloth out, tearing new cloth from her robes, as it was stained. All the while, blood flowed from the open wound.

At first, the blood was mixed with the fluids. At the same time, as Zhao Wan poured that energy into the girl, he felt something shift within her. Not a clearing of meridians, nothing so crass as that, but something deeper.

An echo, as though she, having bathed in his chi, in his understanding of the world had absorbed some portion of it. Feeling the very nature of his Sundering Blade deep within, she had taken up the weapon that was his chi itself and laid it into her flesh and poison.

Energy that should have burnt her to her crisp was guided and wielded, chunks of diseased and rotting flesh coming apart with each moment. By the time the woman was on her third cloth, the wound was clear and the blood coming fresh and red. That was when Zhao Wan stopped pouring energy into the girl.

"Use the energy I gave you now, convert it to yours. Use your energy to take the poison chi and make it quiescent. There is nothing more I can do for you. The rest is up to you."

Having said his piece, Zhao Wan took his hands away from her back. She leaned forward a little, drew a shuddering, pain-filled breath, and set to work. Her meridians thrummed with pain, creaking as they threatened to break under the strain of the too pure, too great energy. Yet each breath, each beat of her heart, the glow around her lessened.

At the same time, the blood slowed and stopped flowing, the wound raw and clear. Zhao Wan wordlessly handed rolls of clean bandages to the aunt, which she used on the young girl even as the man turned his attention to the other infected.

"Honored Benefactor…." His arm raised, his eyes wide and pleading.

"I cannot heal you like her. She is doing all the work and you…" Zhao Wan shook his head. "However, the infection has not spread too far. If I take your arm…"

"Benefactor!" The cry was shocked and outraged, but under Zhao Wan's implacable gaze, the man shrank back.

"Think about it. You have the rest of the night. No longer."

The man offered Zhao Wan a deep bow before scurrying away, leaving the cultivator to regard the surroundings once more. Verifying that not much required his attention, he extracted a simple healing pill suitable for the child and placed it beside her and the aunt. He then took a seat near the fire.

He idly noted that the food in the pot had been consumed, the contents swallowed. His lips quirked a little, wondering if the poison thrown into the fire had infected it. Well, it was too late to worry about it now. He was not sure he would have tried to stop them from consuming the food anyway. The danger of starvation was just as great as the poison.

Eyes closed, he sat and meditated, waiting.

Hours later, Zhao Wan opened his eyes to see the young girl standing before him. She cradled her arm and the pill bottle, staring at him with those serious, clear eyes.

When she saw him look at her, she bowed low. "Thank you, Honored Benefactor."

"You are welcome, young cultivator."

"Honored Benefactor. One question."

"What is it?" Zhao Wan said gently.

"What does quiescent mean?"

Zhao Wan, staring at the girl who was now bound to him by fate and destiny and choice, laughed.

***

Twice that night, he had to see off a prowling Spirit Beast whose greed—or aggressiveness— saw it approach the encampment after tracing the trail of blood back to the camp from the discarded corpses. In both cases, Zhao Wan narrowed his killing intent and thrust it at his opponent, using the sharp edge of his sword dao to damage the creature's aura and spirit. The difference in cultivation level between himself and the creatures was sufficient to drive them away without him wielding his weapon in truth, allowing the exhausted villagers to slumber in peace.

All but two figures.

One, the young girl who sat, cultivating the healing pill he had fed to her. The Marrow and Flesh Cleansing Pill would accelerate both her meridian cleansing and the healing process she was undergoing, though he knew it would leave the young girl ravenous in its wake.

The other figure was the injured man, whose sleep was interrupted by pain, doubt, and indecision. Twice, he approached the silent, meditating cultivator, paused, then scurried away, thinking his actions unseen. Zhao Wan did not need his eyes to note the movement of others around him, not when his spiritual sense was extended. Not when he practiced adjusting to the Thousand Miseries sensory method.

Thankfully, it seemed that the food eaten by the villagers had not been poisoned. Certainly, through the night, the scent of the unwashed, dirty, and sickly villagers did not twist and change as poison burrowed through the lining of their innards to enter their blood stream.

Perhaps it was too mild now to enact such a change. It was something he would have to keep an eye upon as he brought them with him. That decision, he had come to reluctantly. As much as he did not desire to tie himself to this world, he could sense the threads already formed. It had formed when he made the decision to save the girl and, in so doing, tie himself to them.

Whether he chose to abandon them—and thus receive their grievance and anger for forsaking them—or brought them along, he was now bound.

Morning sunlight filtered through the branches and leaves, bringing with it bird song and the stirring of the mortals. Zhao Wan sensed the change in the world around him as nocturnal predators slunk back to their dens and others woke.

In the end, the sick villager came to Zhao Wan, face fixed in grim purpose. The pair left the clearing soon after, only for a scream of pain and loss to punctuate the air shortly after. The final late sleepers in the clearing woke with a start, many clutching one another in fear. Consternation increased as they realized their erstwhile protector was gone, and those with weapons grabbed them, leveling the looted arms against the dense vegetation. Others whispered fearfully amongst one another, some going so far as to approach the meditating child.

Only a last-minute save by the aunt stopped them from disturbing the girl, potentially damaging her meridians as she was abruptly broken from cultivation. Unhappy and fearful, further foolish actions were forestalled by the wash of Zhao Wan's aura pressing upon them, both reassuring and intimidating at the same time.

Eventually, Zhao Wan and the villager returned, the man clutching the stump of his arm by his side. Cries of shock and alarm rang through the clearing once more, though the leading villager just nodded as though a clarifying point had been made.

Soon enough, that same man barked orders again, with foodstuff taken from looted storage rings put to use and a meal set to cooking. Zhao Wan snorted but sat alone, waiting for the mortals to finish their breakfast.

The leader of the villagers arrived soon after, carrying a bowl that he offered to Zhao Wan. Taking the simple meal of congee, roots, and nuts, he held the breakfast close to him while he waited for the man to say what he clearly desired to.

Eventually, the man choked out, "Honored Benefactor, what are your plans for us?"

"Elder Shan Lin of the Forgotten Vale Sect is in that direction." Zhao Wan pointed with two fingers, indicating the direction of travel they would need to take. He noticed the man tense but ignored it as he continued. "It took me two days to find you. I expect it will be a week at least before we make it, at the speed that you and your people will be able to travel." A slight pause, then he added, "Your people will need to forage what meals they can as we travel."

"Thank you. Thank you so much." The man bowed low.

Zhao Wan cocked his head, then realized what the other likely had considered. That they might be abandoned, left to die. A foolish thought, after all he had sacrificed, but not entirely inappropriate.

"A small matter. I must travel that way and that one"—he nodded toward the child—"cannot move at my speed. I have much to do with her."

Again that deep bow from the other man. "If this one can—"

"You cannot. Manage your people well, and we shall call the matter settled. Yes?" Zhao Wan let his voice grow a little sterner. The very last thing he wanted to do was manage the villagers. Keeping them safe was onerous enough.

Once more, the man bowed then backed away. He would have made a good servant, and likely an even better headsman. His ability to read the emotions of his betters would do him well in the future. Zhao Wan almost considered making a note of it to pass the message on to Shan Lin or someone else in power.

Then mentally reeled himself back in. Those kinds of changes might seem innocuous but were often the greatest in life. A single sentence said in the right place or time could set up a man for great fortune or trip him into the pits of despair.

As much as he was interfering in their lives now, Zhao Wan would not sully himself or them with further action. None but a single child, whose future was now intertwined with his. He would have to find a way to cut their connection at some further point. At the least, he would have to ensure her proper placement and care, now that he had set her fate awry.

Now, wouldn't that be an interesting journey in itself?

Chapter 17

Once the villagers were done with their repast, they needed little guidance to begin the trip out of the deep wilds of the kingdom. Where they trod was no-man's-land, a location only the foolhardy or the powerful chose to wander on the regular.

Under his watchful eye, the villagers moved carefully through the undergrowth, holding to as straight a line of travel as they could. Luckily, a single surviving woodsman among the group was able to navigate the undergrowth, bringing the villagers with him. Also fortunate was the lack of a large number of youth, allowing the villagers to make good time.

For mortals.

Unflagging in his optimism and energy, the village headsman moved up and down, chivying those who slowed, offering words of encouragement or a shoulder to lean upon. Zhao Wan knew he lacked the other man's name, but he had no reason to seek it out. And, for reasons of his own, it seemed the man saw no reason to offer it.

Even so, between calls and greetings, Zhao Wan picked out his name soon enough. Chief Hoon moved tirelessly, even as deep lines of worry etched his face. Worries about the future, concerns over feeding the group in the present, and the occasional flash of deep regret and misery as he recalled the past.

"Watch carefully, child." Zhao Wan said to the young girl walking by his side. When they had begun walking, he had beckoned her and her minder over, finally receiving and offering formal introductions to one another. "That is what happens when you take on the burdens of others."

"Yes, Honored Cultivator," Qian Ya Ling said, her voice clear and intelligent.

Now, only the mildest traces of tension could be heard in her voice, if one listened for it.

Tension from being vulnerable in such a dangerous location, from the still healing injury on her arm. From speaking to the cultivator who had swooped down to save them.

"You and I, we walk the path of karma. I intend to cut myself free of all debts, rising to the heavens clear of the niggling bindings of this world," Zhao Wan said. "Your path is one of karma, I can tell. But it diverges as well. Where and how, I know not. That is for you to learn of."

"Karma?" Ya Ling said with a frown. Then she added, "You tell the future, Honored Cultivator?"

"Not if I can help it," Zhao Wan said. "Foretelling is the work of a lax mind, one unable to comprehend the complexity of existence itself and the minor and major changes that a simple decision can create." He gestured down at her. "Your presence here, by my side, is one such." He considered then nodded. "My first lesson then. Consider the multiple paths and decisions, starting from the major to the minor, that brought you here from your village. Start a day before the attack."

"Lesson, Honored Cultivator?"

"Why yes. Did you think I saved your life to just let you waste it?" Zhao Wan's nose wrinkled. "Really. I had not thought you so foolish. I might not take you as an apprentice directly, but you have wasted enough time. If you are to breach the egg of mortality, the time to start growing is now."

"I—"

"Lessons in logic and understanding in the morning. We shall have to delve into the depths of your education. Reading and memorizing the classics is a must. Understanding will come later. In the afternoon, we shall discuss cultivation techniques suitable for yourself, and theory and etiquette among cultivators. In the evenings, we will begin martial training."

"Honored Cultivator… I… this…"

"You should also start calling me Master Cheng. It is more respectful." He inclined his head slightly, considering the words. "Yes. I might be a half-step[9] teacher, but teacher I am."

"But…"

"Well?" He looked down at the girl and then back, for she had slowed and was now behind him.

She clutched her hands together, stilling their trembling by sheer force. "My aunt…" She looked sideways then, at the woman who had cared for her so far.

To Ya Ling's obvious surprise, her aunt was shaking her head already. Seeing both of them staring, she froze. Then, after a moment, her voice shaking just a little, she said, "Go, child.

---

[9] A reference to the fact that he's only halfway teaching her. Used sometimes in our world for (traditional) martial arts teachers and students, it indicates that they are not taught the "true" mysteries and secrets of the art and only taught the basics.

This is an opportunity that your parents—that I—could never dream of offering you. Maybe their deaths, all these deaths, could mean something if you… if you…"

If she what, her aunt never said. Instead, her aunt's eyes scrunched up with tears and she buried her face in her hands. She turned away, ashamed by her outburst of emotion, and Zhao Wan found himself looking aside. The trio hovered uncertainly, until Ya Ling ran to her aunt and wrapped the woman in a tight embrace, her own eyes misty with unshed tears.

They stayed together for a long time. At first, the rest of the villagers had moved ahead, but when they realized that their protector had stopped, they came to a standstill too. However, none of them chose to interrupt the tender moment.

Eventually, the pair pulled apart. The aunt bent down, meeting Ya Ling's all-too-mature gaze, and an unspoken promise passed between them.

When they parted finally, the young girl walked up to Zhao Wan, head held high. "My aunt—"

"Will be taken care of." Zhao Wan cocked his head, considering. "If you join my Sect, she can join us as a servant. Good servants are hard to come by. If you join another, you will have to make arrangements then, but I shall be willing to speak to her devotion and ability."

"Yes, master." She bowed low, casting one last glance at her aunt before she straightened. "But… why not the Verdant Green Waters, master?"

"We have strict requirements for entry," Zhao Wan replied. "Also, your path might not best suit my sect. Karmic paths are not well-favored among the Verdant Green Waters."

He chose not to mention that it was his own interactions with the other Elders that might have soured some of them about karmic daos. Even so, it was not unusual for sects to reject those on such paths. Many karmic daos required specific training, unique cultivation techniques and environments to ensure success. It was no wonder then that small sects that catered to specific ideals of karma and the interaction had sprung up. If not for his own unique situation and his prodigious talent, Zhao Wan himself might have been rejected.

At his gesture, the pair moved once more, catching up to the crowd. After ensuring there were no threats to handle, Zhao Wan stared at the young girl.

"Yes, Master?" she asked.

"Your lesson. Begin."

Another long pause, as she gathered her thoughts. "I woke that morning and chose to do my chores before washing my face. I didn't want my parents to complain about it again. I left the house without telling them…"

Zhao Wan listened as she recited her day step by step. Sometimes backtracking, sometimes jumping around from choice to choice, expanding upon the myriad actions that she could have taken, that her parents could have taken. A lesson in the past and the inconsequential nature of free will and foretelling.

***

Days of walking and using formation flags in the evenings so that they could rest. Even so, the ones Zhao Wan had access to—those he had bought, those he understood from reviewing the documentation held within the formation master's ring that he did not believe trapped— were insufficient for a good night's rest. Most faded away by the early hours of the dawn, unable to hide or contain their presence any longer. Leaving the cultivator to drift, half-awake and watchful for interlopers.

Eight days of fitful nights drew down even the massive stamina of a Core Formation expert, leaving the cultivator increasingly surly by the time they exited the forest. It had not helped that the rainy season had arrived, leaving mortals cold and wet and slow-moving. Of them all, it was only Zhao Wan who managed to stay mostly dry, his ability to prevent the rain from striking him with his aura engendering more than a few envious looks.

In the end, slow though the villagers might have moved, they reached their destination. Towering bamboo trees slowly changed in height, the work of the old village bearing fruit now as more and more light from above was shown. Eventually, the group found themselves moving along a deer trail amidst broken tree stumps and shortened, secondary growth, finally clear of the forest. The group let out a reflexive cheer at that moment, delighted at the signs of nearing civilization.

Once their initial joy at exiting the over-reaching vegetation had subsided, they continued their journey. A location so close to the edge of civilization was not safe, though travel slowed further as exhaustion and tension bled from the group, slowing footsteps with each long moment.

In the end, they managed to make it another li before the village spokesperson called a stop. Even though Zhao Wan pointed out that their destination was only another li and a half away, the distance they had crossed had taken the entire group two hours.

"Understood, Honored Benefactor. But my people, they are not cultivators. They are exhausted. They cannot go farther." The man gestured at the group sprawled around. "Though the meat you have provided has been gratefully received, it has not been sufficient. We were already starved beforehand. This additional travel…"

Zhao Wan sighed, looking at them all. Then he nodded before walking over to his new apprentice. He set her to cultivating while the others prepared the camp. In the meantime, Zhao Wan headed for the ruins.

There was someone who he needed to speak to, a suspicion born of the poisons he held that he wanted to verify. And it would be best that any such verification be done far away from the mortals.

He was not surprised to find Shan Lin still in the remnants of the village. Multiple formation stones had been emplaced around the village, sigils and esoteric paths to control the flow of energy chiseled into their faces. Zhao Wan felt the twisting of the environmental chi as he neared, the formations pulling energy from the village and transforming it with each second.

Yin to yang, while more natural energy flowed in from around, replacing what was lost.

More, as he crested the unnatural hills that had formed around the village, Zhao Wan noted that the opening he had created had been deepened. The earth had been torn up and moved aside to ensure that no water would ever be trapped in that manner again. Ditches and canals had been formed and reinforced around the revealed ruins, while the ground itself slowly dried after the period of heavy rain.

Zhao Wan stood outside the perimeter on the hill, waiting as Shan Lin strolled up from the village. The sun had dropped, the day grown long, and a slight wind having arisen. It was a pleasant day after numerous days of rain and cold. A good day, if not for the upcoming conversation.

"My friend!" Shan Lin waved to Zhao Wan as he neared. "I see you have returned, and not much worse for the wear." His gaze swept over the man, locking onto his clothing and the slight stains on the bottom of his pants and along the edges of his robe. "Though you had some rough times?"

Zhao Wan glanced at the sleeves of his robes, then shrugged. "Laundry is difficult in the wilds. And I have had to deal with a few issues in the meantime."

"Issues?"

"Yes."

Silence stretched between the pair, somewhat uncomfortable as Shan Lin finished his ascent. He frowned a little, cocking his head after a moment. "Well, then? How was your little expedition? Did you learn anything worthwhile?"

"I did. A few things," Zhao Wan said. "Found the ones who were connected to me from here." He gestured back the way they'd come. "Seems like they hadn't realized the village had been flooded. They were making their way here with all new sacrifices."

"Sacrifices?" Shan Lin frowned.

"Villagers. Though they weren't pausing in their experiments on the way here. Whatever data they were trying to gather, it was something even they could see and record," Zhao Wan explained.

"What experiments are you talking about?" Shan Lin asked.

"The poison. The one coming from Elder Tung. They're manipulating it, testing it out," Zhao Wan said. "Using it to try out new variations."

"Diabolical."

"It is."

Silence once more, before Shan Lin cocked his head. "You said the poison coming from Elder Tung. Don't you mean infecting him?"

"Yes."

"Zhao Wan…" Shan Lin said.

"What I don't understand is why."

"Why what?" The older man shifted his position, stroking his mustache now. One arm wrapped around his torso, hand hanging over the edge of one sword breaker.

"Why save me?" Zhao Wan said. "I was caught in a trap of my own making. If you hadn't pulled me out, I would have flayed my soul myself with that formation. All you needed to do was step aside."

"What are you suggesting, my friend?" Shan Lin said softly. "That I have a reason to see you dead?"

"Not you individually, perhaps. But your organization? Certainly. You let me find your people, let me kill them. Why?"

"So. You really think I am part of this mysterious organization poisoning my friend, letting him die slowly. Do you think I'm so base?"

"That's the first time you've ever called Elder Tung your friend. Weeks together, and you never once said that," Zhao Wan said.

"Did I not?" Shan Lin made a face. "You're right. A mistake. I should have been more careful." He laughed. "But really, I always thought you'd join us. Once I laid it out, dropped the hints, brought you in slowly. After all, you already walk a path similar to ours."

"And what path is that?" Zhao Wan asked, still standing patiently. Relaxed.

"We have no name, not for those who aren't part of us. Not yet. You can say we walk a darker path, one different even from the heretics. We bow to no one, no heaven, no hells. No demons. Why chain ourselves to others when we can climb to the peak ourselves?"

"And the poison? What has that got to do with any of this?" Zhao Wan gestured down to the village. "All this killing for what purpose?"

Shan Lin shrugged.

"What does that mean?" Now, Zhao Wan's voice dropped, a dangerous killing edge coming to it.

"It means what it means. I was never part of this plan. Didn't care for it then, don't care for it now." He laughed. "Let them play. It bothers me not." Zhao Wan growled, and Shan Lin grinned. "But I can guess. Do you want me to guess?"

Zhao Wan hesitated before he nodded, eyes narrowed as he tried to judge if the other was mocking him. Or just lying.

"Simple really. Some of our leaders, they're not content at just ascending and being set apart from heaven or the hells. No. They want to be on top even here." He cocked his head, a tight smile crossing his face. Not a nice one, but one filled with long-born malice. "Why shouldn't they? After all, the Verdant Green Waters stands above us all, shading out all the other sects, all the other cultivators in this kingdom. Taking away all the resources, hiding all the cultivation techniques.

"So better to burn it all down. Or climb to the top. Either or."

Zhao Wan looked away to where the villagers were. Then back down toward the village and the cemetery that had been cleansed. How he might not have clued in on the jiangshi's origins if he had not found that single hidden corpse. Or maybe just charted that mystery for another person to deal with.

Just like the myriad problems he had let Shan Lin handle while on their way here.

"Did you think I'd just ignore it all? Maybe come here, hunt around, and go back?"

"That was the initial hope." Shan Lin said. "Then, maybe you'd lose the others after your little foretelling. After all, you said it yourself. Such methods are never certain."

"And in the meantime, you'd what? Still see if I am someone you can convince to join you?"

"Yes. Won't you?" the older cultivator asked, arching an eyebrow. "You care little for the mortals. They are but encumbrances to your dao path. Why not join us, carve your way to the top? Cut your soul free from sect and morality."

Silence greeted those words, his last sentence said with almost a shout. Shan Lin grinned, that good-natured smile now turning darker, more bloodthirsty. Then he lowered his arms, staring at the boy before him. Waiting for his answer.

"A tempting offer," Zhao Wan said eventually, and Shan Lin began to smile. "But for one thing."

"What's that?"

Zhao Wan touched the hilt of his blade then, slipping his hand around to grip it. Shan Lin tensed, putting his hands on his sword breakers.

"I intend to cut myself free of all ties. Including those to you and your organization."

Chapter 18

From the first clash, when Zhao Wan drew his jian and had his sword blocked, he was pushed back by Shan Lin. The man's sword breakers seemed to have multiplied in number, coming at Zhao Wan from disparate angles and at a significantly higher speed than before. Every attempt at regaining his balance or the tempo of the fight was noted and blocked by the other before it was completed. Every stroke of his jian was foreseen, his style, his technique now an open book to the other.

The Scholar's Refusal saw his blade smashed into his own ribs by a riposting parry. The Second Call never materialized, the simple disengage and wrist strike struck down by overwhelming force. The Hero's Fall saw him tumbling as the earth itself moved beneath his feet, slipping away as he lowered his weight.

Rolling down the steep slope of the hill, he came to a crunching stop as a stone embankment rose up behind his falling body, arresting his descent and driving his breath from his lungs. As he struggled upward, he barely managed to raise his sword in a flat-bladed, two-handed block against descending paired sword breakers.

Blade biting into his palm, his body crushed against cultivator-reinforced and created stone, Zhao Wan felt his ribs crack as Shan Lin poured energy through the attack, forcing it past his own aura defenses into Zhao Wan's body.

"Thought you were so good, did you not, boy? That you could mock me while fighting?" Shan Lin crowed, a frenzied look in his eyes as he pressed down both blades, forcing the heavy weapons toward Zhao Wan. The attack poured chi through the connection, cracking Zhao Wan's aura and sending the energy invading the man's meridians and muscles. "I was testing you, boy!"

The two rectangular blades descended farther, a cackling dark energy forming around them as ever more chi was poured into the weapons. Zhao Wan cursed, his arms trembling as he fought against both the physical and chi-based attacks. As energy poured from Shan Lin, a dark, cloying scent that was slightly rancid and twisted formed around the earth energy, as though a badly managed compost pile had been turned after an age.

Distracted, Shan Lin's blades crept closer to Zhao Wan's skin, the rippling energy touching his aura directly at his shoulders. He felt it invade his meridians, intent on corrupting and damaging. Zhao Wan's lips pulled back into a snarl, trapped as he was against the unyielding stone. All his vaunted skill and expertise beaten by untamed ferocity and aggression.

Such a stupid way to die.

That thought emboldened Zhao Wan. He would not die here and now. He would not let his story end over a simple misjudgment. He would not be thrown back into that damn cycle to be a victim of karma once again.

He. Would. Not.

Energy poured out of his dantian. There was a difference here, in strength between he who had a single layer in his Core and the man he fought against. There was no way Zhao Wan could contest the sheer amount of energy battering at him.

So he did not.

Blade intent poured into his chi, and he turned it on the energy streaming from his body. Angled it such that it tore through the obstruction in his back, ripping apart the reinforced earth barrier that held him prey to his opponent.

Reinforced stone was sliced apart by sharpened blade intent and cracked under the immense pressure put upon it. Zhao Wan flew backward, tumbling head over heels down the hill as his opponent stumbled, his paired weapons smashing into the remnants of the stone and exploding them. Dust and pebbles rained down from the point of impact, even as Zhao Wan caught his fall and threw himself aside into a new angle of retreat.

Not a moment too soon, as Shan Lin leapt to where Zhao Wan had been, his sword breakers thrust before him to smash unsuspecting bodies. He moved well past Zhao Wan, coming to a stop soon after, a giant rent in earth forming as he stopped. The empowered stone attack he had created was released, the energy tearing into remnant buildings in the buried village, sending even more walls tumbling to the earth.

"Now look what you've made me do," Shan Lin said, shaking his head. "You should just have died, rather than make me destroy more of my work."

Zhao Wan looked at the torn earth and spotted numerous buried formation stones. A half-dozen revealed, each meticulously carved and buried prior to his arrival.

A trap then.

It did not matter. He raised his sword into a mid-guard only to frown as he spotted the heavily chipped edge. A problem when wielding a simple Spirit weapon, a grade lower than his opponent's. He had not had the time to upgrade it, nor the resources since his ascension to Elder.

A mistake that might cost him his life.

Exhale. Inhale. Focus.

Zhao Wan's opponent was stalking toward him now, moving slower. Like a rumbling landslide that had just begun, picking up speed with each step. To face such an attack…

Zhao Wan shifted his stance, readying himself for the first form. Karma Severing Cut. Dangerous to use again, what with his soul, aura, and dantian already shredded by the attacks, by his own mistakes. But the other man outmatched him in strength, in endurance, in cunning.

Better to finish this fast.

Hand held mid-height, blade low, he gathered the energy, sharpening his dao intent.

As though expecting the action, Shan Lin charged Zhao Wan, surfing across the ground on a platform of solid earth that crossed the space between the pair in moments. He rode forward, a barrier of earth rising up to meet and join the shell of earth, a shell that sparkled and twisted as metal solids formed around it too. Deep within, the entire formation was reinforced by even more energy.

A protection against Zhao Wan's attack that breached most defenses. He felt the formations created in this shell that came from the earth, that had been carved into small stones and left all through this land. Just for this moment.

All in preparation for him to launch his attack and see it break. Perhaps even rebound again, crippling him forever.

His intent had been anticipated. Just like his earlier forms. But this did not stop Zhao Wan as he cut upward, throwing the entirety of the formed energy into the single motion, such that his blade strike was one of white, arced energy laced with killing intent.

It impacted the shell Shan Lin had created, shattering it apart and revealing the cultivator. The immense attack that Zhao Wan had formed could not break the defense, only reveal the man within. However, formations meant to block a karmic attack failed to trigger as the attack contained only blade intent and core chi.

There was no panic in Shan Lin's eyes as he stared at Zhao Wan. Already, more formation stones were flying through the air or were being pulled up from the ground. The earth shield Shan Lin had created was also reforming, protecting him again.

Obviously, he had not expected Zhao Wan to fall into every one of his traps. It was enough to be protected now.

Then Shan Lin's eyes widened as Zhao Wan's rising blade stopped, his wrist turned, and the energy—the dao intent—that he had been gathering, that Zhao Wan had not dispersed sharpened and flowed into the blade. Joining the reformed blade energy that he wielded to impart the attack as he cut down once more.

The second cut did not have the strength of the first. There was no way to reform that much energy after expending it all in that brief motion. The cut was a weak, pitiful thing in terms of blade energy, something a newly trained Energy Storage cultivator might create.

But the dao intent within was still there.

The Sundering Blade flowed forward, crossing the distance between the pair before it impacted Shan Lin's reforming protective earth wall.

And there was no formation to hinder it.

The attack entered the cultivator's body, passed through him, and exited without leaving a mark. At least, not externally. Yet a moment later, the earth shell fell apart, the body flopping down bonelessly within the crumbling earth and entombed within, the entire assembly sliding to a stop before Zhao Wan's feet.

Quiet filled the abandoned village once more, only the settling earth and the far-off cry of a soaring bird filling the dead air.

Zhao Wan inhaled sharply and winced at the bones that pressed into his back. He sheathed his blade and then, staring at the still body, spoke. Softly.

"Second form of the Sundering Blade. Soul Severing Cut."

Funny, that his second form never saw the heavens reproach him. Perhaps because that action was not against their dictates. Freeing a soul to pass on to the next life, rather than freeing it from the binds of karma itself.

A small difference.

A massive change.

Chapter 19

"Is this where you intend to deliver me, Master?"

The question broke Zhao Wan from his thoughts, bringing his attention to the present. He looked down at Ya Ling, clad in simple peasant robes still—though newer and cleaner than the ones she had worn after he had purchased them at a passing village—and marveled again at the uncommon poise and calmness she had. For an adult, she would have been excellent. For a child, she was magnificent.

"No. The one I intend for you is far away. I told you that already," Zhao Wan said, his voice a little annoyed.

"But we've been walking for so long already. Months and months!" Ya Ling said.

"It has not been months," Zhao Wan said. "Just a few weeks. And it would have been faster if you'd learned the movement techniques properly."

"It is so tiring, Master." Ya Ling rubbed her bum surreptitiously.

"Of course it is. Your muscles are not built for it yet. You will learn though," Zhao Wan said. "Anyway, we'll soon be taking boats and canals the rest of the way. It isn't much faster, but it does require less focus. You can spend more time cultivating then."

Ya Ling looked as though she might have something to say about that, but she shook her head a little. She straightened her robes, smoothing them down, then nodded in acceptance, tiny lips fixed firmly. She turned her gaze back to the tower-like structure, her eyes drifting over the multiple floors and the upturned roof edges. "Why are we here then, Master? If this is not our destination?"

"Not your destination," Zhao Wan said. "It is mine. I'm here to cut a thread finally."

She nodded as if she comprehended what he meant. Perhaps she did. He had told her about his dao path in the hopes it would clarify her own. She was too young still to truly grasp her path, but the sect he intended for her to join would continue the training he had begun. At the least, they would recognize that she was on a similar path and ensure she traversed it properly.

Doing that, he hoped, would help reduce the thread that had grown between them. Even now, he could feel it pull and twist between them.

"I will have you wait out here. You are within sight of the Protector, so you will be in no danger." Zhao Wan gestured to a nearby hut which the farmers used to store bags of rice and their tools during the growing months. "Continue cultivating. You should have broken through another meridian by now, after all the aid you have been given."

He felt her tense a little at his words before she forcibly made herself relax. Once more, he wondered at the life that she'd had that she had learned such great control at a young age. It rarely came from a happy family life. Yet he would not ask. He had no desire to learn it, beyond basic curiosity and that was insufficient to tangle their lives further.

Ya Ling bowed and murmured, while her head was lowered, "I will do my best, Master."

Of course, he did not tell her that he noticed the tongue she stuck out at him when her head was bowed. Not yet, at least. Let her have her minor rebellions and minor lies. Later, he would explain in detail how strong his spiritual sense was.

Zhao Wan knew he was being harsh on her. Expecting her to break through another meridian by now was entirely unfair, but strict discipline and high expectations would drive her to greater heights than conciliatory words and lax rules.

Once she had taken a seat, placing the smaller backpack she had been assigned for her personal items beside her, Zhao Wan left. He took care to move using the basic form of the Wind Steps system, offering her an opportunity to review his technique and correct her own mistakes. It was significantly slower than he could have moved, but it did not matter. Their objective was only a li away.

By the time he arrived at the tower, he knew that both Protector and Patriarch had sensed his presence. The Patriarch had even opened his aura a little, allowing his location to be sensed by Zhao Wan. A quiet invitation for him to discuss matters.

Zhao Wan chose not to take up the unspoken invitation. Instead, he turned toward the infirmary, treading between the emptied-out beds as he made way inward. Only a half-dozen patients were left, those still too injured to travel back to their villages, and a single new patient.

The pair of inner sect cultivators who worked the infirmary glanced at Zhao Wan as he made his way through the room, but neither spoke with him. After all, the man wore the robes of a Verdant Green Waters Sect Elder. And while the various sect robes might be easily forgettable, the one for the premier sect in the kingdom was likely burnt into their minds.

It also, probably, helped that Zhao Wan moved with the unconscious grace of a predator at the moment. Heading directly for the small room set aside for Physician Gu, he never managed to finish his journey before the woman herself cut him off.

"Elder Cheng. What brings you toward me with such a strident purpose? Retract your aura better, boy. You are scaring my patients."

Zhao Wan cocked his head, noting how she came out aggressively. Just like the last time. The first time, he had reacted negatively, accepting her abuse as though he'd deserved it. Now though, he saw it for the tactic that it was.

"Tell me. How long have you been working against your very own sect?" Time to match blade with blade.

"What rubbish do you speak of? If you intend to insult me, leave."

"Do not try to dissemble. Your compatriot gave you up while we fought." Zhao Wan shook his head almost sadly. "Always a big speaker, he was. Do you not think so?"

"You continue to speak rubbish. Leave now, I have patients to attend to," Physician Gu said heatedly. She waved one hand at him while the other one stayed by her side, the palm turned away from Zhao Wan.

"Like Lord Ye being fond of dragons[10], you and your patients." Zhao Wan said. "I did not

---

10 叶公好龙 (yè gōng hào long)—literally translates as Lord Ye is fond of dragons. An idiom that comes from the storied Lord Ye, a court magistrate, who used to have dragon carvings and images in everything he owned. A real dragon, enamored with someone who loved them so much, came to visit Lord Ye. At that point, Lord Ye hid, for he was actually afraid of the dragon. As such, it can be said that

need Elder Shan's confession anyway. I had the evidence I need."

"Evidence!" She snorted. "Then show it."

In answer, Zhao Wan raised his right hand, pulling one of the poison bottles into his hand. He held the pill bottle between his thumb and finger to show it to the Physician, all while watching her reaction. In the back of his mind, he felt the shift in aura, the turning of attention to the pair as they spoke.

"A pill bottle. That's your evidence?" she scoffed.

"A pill bottle containing a poison. A familiar-smelling poison."

"So, you found the source of the poison. Well done. But why accuse me of misdeeds? Because it comes in a pill bottle?"

---

he liked the image or thought of dragons, but not the real thing. Or "pretending to like something" or "pretending to care for something when one doesn't."

Zhao Wan shook his head. "You are very good at acting outraged, but did you know that calligraphy strokes are like sword strokes? They all have a unique feature to them."

Reaching his other hand out sideways, he pulled a nearby pill bottle from where it rested, waiting for application from a patient, letting the chi tendrils he wielded bring it to him. Snatching the bottle out of the air, he turned both around to showcase the sloppy calligraphy to the Physician.

"Your handwriting, is it not?" Zhao Wan said.

There was a period of tense stillness as she regarded the two pill bottles. Then she moved, flicking the hand she had been hiding in a wide arc. A spray of acupuncture needles, each coated with a poison, flew from her hand.

Zhao Wan cursed, for he realized the moment she moved that she had not been targeting just him but also the patients and the inner sect cultivators within the room. He could not let them be harmed, or he would suffer the karmic consequences of his own arrogance.

Waving his hands, he conjured quick flashes of blade intent with his chi, using bare hands to wield the attacks. Without a sword, the blade crescents were less powerful; but he was a master of the jian, a man who had achieved the Heart of the Sword. He would have no face if he could not deal with a dozen poisoned needles without his sword.

Of course, by the time he finished with that, Physician Gu had fled into her room, shutting the door behind her and locking it. That, in itself, would not have stopped him. The teetering jar set next to the door, ready to be pushed aside or broken at the barest movement, did.

No telling what kind of poison she had slipped into that jar, or the effects it would have on the mortals. Anyway, he could tell she was fleeing out the window, out of the tower itself.

"Run all you like, but you will not be able to outrun me," Zhao Wan murmured, turning on his heels.

Only to be brought to a stop in surprise, for another figure, one he had not noticed arriving, stood behind him.

"Was what you said true?" the Patriarch demanded, his eyes burning with fury.

"See for yourself," Zhao Wan said, gesturing to the bottles that had fallen to the floor.

The Patriarch snatched them up, staring at the words written in an all-too-familiar scrawl. He popped open their covers, sniffing at both and grimacing, covering them immediately after. The thunderous look on his face grew even more pronounced, and he shot Zhao Wan a look that could freeze bones.

"You will not chase her."

"Patriarch…!"

"This is now an internal matter. We shall deal with her." The Patriarch's lips curled up in a snarl. "I shall handle the matter. Personally."

Zhao Wan hesitated, staring at the enraged older man and balancing his own needs and sensibilities against the other man's fury. Pushing matters now…

"Of course." Zhao Wan bowed. "You will keep me and my Sect informed?"

"I will." The Patriarch hesitated before he gestured upward. "Elder Tung has been succumbing to the poison faster, ever since you arrived. I had thought it was a coincidence but now…"

"Perhaps he can recover, now that she is not managing his care?" Zhao Wan offered hopefully.

"No. It is too late. See for yourself. In fact, I insist you do. Speak to him, finish your business. And then leave." The Patriarch shook his head. "Your aid in solving this mystery is gratefully received, but your presence is no longer welcome."

Zhao Wan bowed low in acknowledgment. He understood. He was a living, breathing marker of the Patriarch's failure to see what had been happening within his own sect. No man who'd achieved the heights he had would want such a reminder around.

By the time Zhao Wan came out of his bow, the Patriarch had left in the same manner as he had arrived. And somehow, Zhao Wan found himself pitying the physician when the man finally caught her.

***

The smell coming from the room was overpowering. Even without activating the Thousand Miseries technique, Zhao Wan found himself holding a scented handkerchief to his nose as he entered Elder Tung's room.

His benefactor was naught but skin and bone now, the disease having drained him of strength and fat in equal measure. His hair, once lustrous and plentiful, was stringy and much of it fallen out. The wound on his side was covered, but the dark, necrotic liquid soaked the bandages even now, tendrils extending from the infection past where the bandages ended.

Each breath was raspy, filled with phlegm, and irregular, as though the next breath was but an afterthought for a still struggling spirit. The man's lips were dry and cracked, bleeding edges whistling with each breath.

Zhao Wan felt a surge of sympathy and looked around, searching for someone, anyone who should have been here for the man now. In the last few moments of his life, he was alone. Elder Tung had never had an apprentice, never had a family like most cultivators. But surely someone in his sect would be here…

Yet, there were none.

A part of Zhao Wan wanted to curse the sect, to demand that they do better for the old man who had given the sect so much. Yet who was he to demand one to tie themselves to another? When he had chosen to cut himself loose from such mortal frailties himself?

And yet...

Picking up a teacup and a clean cloth, he poured a little of the liquid on the cloth before cleaning the man's lips. Then he edged the man's neck upward a little and poured a small amount of the tea into the parched throat. Through all this, Elder Tung did not stir, his breathing still labored and difficult.

"I... I'm sorry. I wish I could have found the solution earlier. Noticed things faster. If I had, perhaps..." Zhao Wan was unsure what else to say. Would it have made a difference? Or had it been too late ever since Elder Tung had been poisoned?

What had been the process of this? Had Elder Tung really been injured by a beast to begin with? Or had the Physician or Elder Shan poisoned him on purpose? Was he used to inculcate the poison, his Core Formation constitution allowing the dark sect to test and extract the poisons from the wound in his side? That was, after all, what each of those bottles with their dates had been for. Extracts taken across multiple days.

Perhaps Zhao Wan would learn the answer when the Patriarch caught the physician. He hoped so. For Shan Lin had hinted at an organization that was not content to attack a single sect. A group, a dark sect, that sought to pull down the orthodox sects and become the rulers in their place.

It was a foreboding thought.

"Well, I did find your poisoner. I did learn what was going on. It was rather simple, at the end of the day…" Zhao Wan said, telling the unconscious Elder what had happened. What he'd learned. What he assumed. And finally, the confrontation and the Patriarch's orders.

"So I guess… this is the end of my trip here. I think I've done what you asked." He felt within, touching the thread that had dissolved a little. Just a little… "Or perhaps not."

Now Zhao Wan felt a flicker of anger. Was this not enough? Was finding the culprit insufficient to balance the scales? To cut himself free of the old man?

"Or what was it that you asked? To save the orthodox sects?" Zhao Wan found himself leaning back, almost laughing. "Is this, is this what you planned, you damn old man? To tie me to saving the sects?"

He threw away the cloth in disgust, standing and walking away from the insensate form. Zhao Wan stalked up and down the room, opening and closing his mouth as he sought the words, the energy to shout at the unconscious man.

Eventually though, he flopped down in the chair he had taken in the beginning, arms crossed.

"What is the worth of a single life?" Zhao Wan shook his head. "Very well. I'll work to save the orthodox sects. Until this damn thread is cut and my obligation finished." Then, impishly, he added, "Or I learn how to cut the thread without doing all this work."

There was no reply but another thready breath in. Then a slight pause before the breath flowed out. Zhao Wan stared at the body, waiting for the next long breath, another statement, another declaration of intent running through his mind. But the next breath never came.

The cultivator walked over and placed a hand on his benefactor's neck. No pulse. He considered trying to aid him, pour chi, the very life force that ran through him and the world into Elder Tung. But what was the point? To bring back his benefactor to more agony, more pain?

No.

He removed his hand, straightened Elder Tung's clothing, and pulled the blanket to cover the man and make him a little more presentable. Then Zhao Wan called for aid, to allow the sect to do with the body as they wished. His obligation to the man was over. At least his obligation to the body.

As for his promise, for the thread that stretched between him and Elder Tung's soul downward into a place Zhao Wan could not see, to one of the many hells, that still held strong.

For what worth was a single life saved from the clutches of evil? To what degree would he have to act against this unknown opponent, from now and into the future?

Cheng Zhao Wan did not know, but he understood that it would consume much of his future. He could not see the ends of this path, but he could feel the reverberations of it through all the threads of karma that tied him to this world, to the fate that existed for him and hundreds of others.

And he knew that this was but the beginning.

###

The End of The Sundering Blade

Read more about an older, wiser Master Cheng and the apprentice he takes on in *A Thousand Li: the First Step*.

Turn the page for a sneak peek of the first chapter.

And if you're interested in their first meeting, take a look in Ten Thousand and One Fates.

A Thousand Li: the First Step Deluxe Edition

Mark your calendars for April 2024 as *A Thousand Li: the First Step* is getting a deluxe edition to celebrate the series' five-year anniversary!

Don't want to miss the launch of this one-of-a-kind edition?

Sign up for notifications on Starlit Publishing:

https://starlitpublishing.com/products/the-first-step-deluxe-edition

Preview of A Thousand Li: the First Step
Chapter 1

"Cultivation, at its core, is a rebellion."

Waiting for their reaction, the thin, mustached older teacher stared at the students seated cross-legged before him. Apparently not seeing the reaction he wanted, the teacher flung the long, trailing sleeves of the robes he wore with a harrumph and continued his lecture. Keeping his expression entirely neutral, Long Wu Ying could not help but smirk within. Such a statement, no matter how contentious, lost its impact after daily repetition over the course of a decade.

"Cultivation demands one to defy the very heavens itself. Each step on the path of cultivation sets you on the road to rebellion to defy the heavens, to defy our king. It is only by his good graces and his belief in the betterment of the kingdom that you are allowed to cultivate."

Wu Ying struggled to keep his face neutral as the refrain continued. Usually, he could tune out the teacher until it came time to cultivate, but today he struggled to do so. Today, he could not help but rebut the teacher in his mind. Teaching the villagers how to cultivate was a purely practical decision on the king's part. Most children would achieve at least the first level of Body Cleansing by their twelfth birthday. That allowed them to grow stronger and healthier, even on the little food they had left after the state, the nobles, and the sects had taken their portion.

"The beneficent auspices of the king allow you to cultivate, study the martial arts, and defend yourself. It is only because of his belief that each village must be a strong member of the kingdom that we have grown to the heights we have!"

It had nothing to do with the desire to begin training the villagers to be useful soldiers in the never-ending wars. Or to ensure that the village was not robbed of the grain they farmed by the bandits that seemed to grow in number every year. Or the fact that less than two hundred li[11] away, the Verdant Green Waters Sect watched over them all, searching for new recruits.

"Now, begin!"

Exhaling a grateful breath that Master Su had finally finished, Wu Ying tried to focus his mind on cultivating. That he respected his teacher was without question, but Master Su was a stickler for the rules, which required him to give the same lecture every single time. Even a saint would find it hard to listen after a while. And Wu Ying was many things, but a Saint he most definitely was not.

---

[11] Half a kilometer or roughly a third of a mile

It didn't help that the state was obviously of two minds about cultivation itself. The three pillars of a kingdom were the government, the populace, and the cultivating sects. A weakness in any of the three would make a kingdom vulnerable. For a kingdom to be stable, each pillar needed to be as strong, as upright and firm, as the others. If any single pillar grew too high, it would eventually lead to the collapse of the kingdom.

Because of that, a wise ruler would support the development of their populace through cultivation, the surest and best form of developing an individual. But a single cultivator, if they achieved true power, could—and had, historically—overturn governments. And so, the state would always view cultivators and cultivation with some degree of distrust.

"Wu Ying. Focus!" Master Su said.

Wu Ying grimaced slightly before he made his face placid again. Master Su was right. He could think about all these thoughts another time. This was the time for cultivation. The time a villager had to cultivate was limited and precious. Stray thoughts were wasteful.

Drawing a deep breath, Wu Ying exhaled through his nose. The first step in cultivation was to clear the mind. The second was to control his breathing, for breath was the source of all things. At least in the Yellow Emperor's Cultivation Method that had been passed down and used by all peasants in the kingdom of Shen.

The first step on the road to cultivation was that of bodily purification. To ascend, to gain greater strength and develop one's chi, a cultivator needed to purify their body of the wastes that accumulated. Starting the process young helped to reduce the amount of such waste build up and speeded up the progress of cultivation. That was why every villager began cultivating as soon as possible. Those children who achieved the first level of Body Cleansing at a young age were hailed as prodigies.

Wu Ying was not considered a prodigy. Wu Ying had started cultivating at the age of six, like every other child in the village, and through hard work and discipline, he'd managed to achieve not just the first level of Body Cleansing but the second. True prodigies, at Wu Ying's age of seventeen, would already be at the fourth or fifth stage. Each of the twelve stages of Body Cleansing saw the conscious introduction and cleansing of another major chi meridian. When an individual had consciously introduced and could control the flow of chi through all twelve major pathways, all the stages of Body Cleansing were considered complete.

Wu Ying breathed in then out, slowly and rhythmically. He focused on the breath, the flow of air into his lungs, the way it entered his body as his stomach expanded and his chest filled out. Then he exhaled, feeling his stomach contract, the diaphragm moving upward as air circulated away.

In time, Wu Ying moved his focus away from breathing toward his dantian. Located below his belly button, in the space just slightly below his hip line and a few inches beneath the surface of his body, the lower dantian was the core of the Yellow Emperor's Cultivation Method. From there, through the flow and consolidation of one's internal chi, one would progress.

Once again, Wu Ying felt the mass of energy that was his dantian. As always, it was large in size but low in density, uncompacted and diffuse. His job was to gently nudge the flow of energy through his body's meridians, to send it on a major circulation through his body. In the process, his body sweated, as the normally docile chi moved through his body, cleansing and scouring away the impurities of life. In time, Wu Ying's normal sweat mixed with the impurities in his body, flowing from his pores. The rancid, bitter odor from Wu Ying's body mixed with the similar pungence coming from the rest of the class, a stench that even the open windows of the building could do little to disperse.

***

Deep in the process of cultivating, none of the students noticed the rancid smell, leaving only Master Su to suffer as he watched over the teenagers. Master Su had long gotten used to the offensive odor that he would be forced to endure for the next few hours as each of the classes progressed. It was a fair trade though, for Master Su received ten tael[12] of silver and, most importantly, a Marrow Cleansing pill each month for his work.

Deep in their cultivation, none of the students moved when a young man shook and

---

[12] A measurement of weight. Roughly 37.5 grams

convulsed. But Master Su took action, flashing over to the boy with a tap of his foot. Paired fingers raised as Master Su studied the thrashing boy before they darted forward, striking in rapid succession a series of acupressure points along the body. After the third strike, the convulsing slowed then stopped before the boy tipped over, coughing out blood.

"Foolish. Pushing to open the second meridian channel when you have not finished cleansing the first!" Master Su berated the boy, shaking his head. "Get up. Begin cultivating properly. You will stay here an extra hour."

"But…" the boy protested weakly but quieted at Master Su's glare.

"Foolish child!" Master Su growled as he stomped back to his station in front of the class. If he had not been there, the boy would likely have damaged himself permanently. Master Su watched as the boy wiped his mouth clear of blood before he snorted. Luckily, Master Su had been able to quell the rampaging chi flow, but the boy would likely have to spend the next few weeks on light duty at his farm. A bad time for that, considering the planting season they were in. "Stupid."

As the hour set aside for the teenagers to cultivate came to an end and the morning sun cast long shadows on the small village, the village bell rang. Master Su frowned slightly then smoothed his face as the students broke free from their cultivation trances one by one. It would never do for the students to see his concern.

"The session is over. Line up when you are done," Master Su commanded before he walked out of the small, single-room building that made up his school.

Outside, the teacher walked forward slightly, turning his head from side to side before he spotted the growing dust cloud.

"Master Su." Tan Cheng, the tall village head, came up to Master Su.

As the two individuals in the sixth level of the Body Cleansing stage, the pair shared the burden of guarding the village from external threats. It helped that Chief Tan was a lover of tea like Master Su.

"Chief Tan," Master Su greeted. "What is it?"

"The army recruiters," Chief Tan said, his eyes grave.

Master Su could not help but wince. This was the third time in as many years that the army had recruited from their village. The conscripts from the first year had yet to return, though news of deaths had trickled back. The war between their state of Shen and the state of Wei had dragged on, bringing misery to everyone.

"They're going to raise the taxes again then," Master Su said, trying to keep his tone light. Each year that the war dragged on, the taxes grew higher. He wondered how many the army would take this time and did not envy his friend. The first time the army arrived, they had filled the requirements with volunteers. The second time they came, each household that had more than one son and had yet to send a volunteer had sent their sons. This time, there would be no easy choices.

"Most likely." Chief Tan chewed on his lip slightly. As the rest of the villagers slowly streamed in from the surrounding fields, he looked around then looked down, avoiding the expectant gazes of the parents. Whatever came next, few would be happy.

***

"What is it?" Qiu Ru asked. The raven-haired beauty of the class prodded Wu Ying in the back as she tried to peer past the crowd of students who had gathered around the windows. Giving up, she prodded Wu Ying once more in the back to get him to answer.

"The army," Wu Ying finally answered.

As her eyes widened, he admired the way it made them shine—before he squashed his burgeoning feelings again. Qiu Ru had made it quite clear last summer festival that she had no interest in him. Now, Wu Ying had his sights set on Gao Yan. Even if Gao Yan was shorter, plumper, and had a bad tendency to forget to brush her teeth. That was life in the village—your choices were somewhat limited.

"Are they bringing back the volunteers?" Qiu Ru said.

"No. They're too early for that," Cheng Fa Hui said.

Wu Ying glanced at his friend, who had hung back with the rest of them. Not that Fa Hui needed to be up front to see what was happening. He towered over the entire group by a head. All except Wu Ying, who only lost to him by a handbreadth.

"If the army was returning our people, it would be before the winter," Fa Hui said. "That way the lord would not need to feed them."

Wu Ying grimaced and shot a look around the room, relaxing slightly when he saw that Yin Xue had not come to class today. As the nearest village to Lord Wen's summer abode, all the villagers dealt with Lord Wen and his son regularly. Truth be told, Yin Xue did not need to come to their village class, but the boy seemed to take pleasure in showcasing his ability over the peasants. As the son of the local lord, Yin Xue had access to a private cultivation tutor, spiritual herbs, and good food—all of which had allowed him to progress to Body Cleansing four already. In common parlance, he was what was known as a false dragon—a "forced" genius, rather than one who had achieved the heights of his cultivation by genius alone.

If Yin Xue had heard Fa Hui… Wu Ying mentally shuddered at the thought. Still, it was not as if Fa Hui was wrong. If the war was over, it made sense to make the villagers feed the returned sons rather than pay for hungry mouths over the winter.

"Are they here for us then?" Wu Ying mused. That would make sense.

After saying the words out loud, he noticed how the rest of the class stiffened. Before he could say anything to comfort them, Master Su called them out of the building.

Once the students had lined up outside, Wu Ying could easily see the army personnel, two of which were speaking with Chief Tan, while the others watched over the conscripts. As it was still early in the morning, the army had only managed to visit one other village thus far, and as such, there were only twenty such conscripts standing together. Yin Xue sat astride a horse, beside the conscripts but not part of them.

Wu Ying had to admit, the members of the army looked dashing in their padded undercoats, dark lamellar armor, and open-faced helms. But having watched two other groups leave and not return, with only rumors of the losses trickling back via the same recruiters and the itinerant merchant, much of the prestige and glory of joining the army had faded.

"Men, Lord Wen has sent his men to us once again. We are required to send twenty strong conscripts to join the king's army this year." Before the crowd could grasp the significance of the number, Chief Tan announced, "All sons from families who have not sent a child to the front, step forward."

Wu Ying stepped forward. As the only surviving son of his family, he had been safe from the recruiters beforehand. Along with Wu Ying, another six men stepped forward.

"All sons from families with more than one son in the village, step forward," Chief Tan announced.

This time, there was some confusion, but it was soon sorted out with some students pushed forward and others drawn back. By now, Wu Ying counted seventeen "volunteers."

"Why not daughters?" Qiu Ru called.

Wu Ying could not help but grimace at her impertinent words. As the local beauty, Qiu Ru had managed to get away with more impertinent comments than others. Interrupting the Chief while he was speaking was a new high.

"The army is looking for men!" Chief Tan snapped. "Qiu Jan! See to your daughter!"

"This is foolish!" Qiu Ru said.

When Chief Tan began to speak, he was silenced by a raised hand of the lieutenant, whose gaze raked over Qiu Ru. "You are quite the beauty. But our men do not need wives."

The hiss from the crowd was loud even as Qiu Ru flushed bright red at the insult.

"We are here to find soldiers. And you are, what? Body Cleansing one? Women are no use to us as soldiers until at least Body Cleansing four!"

Still flushed, Qiu Ru moved to speak, but her mother had managed to make her way over to the impertinent girl and gripped her arm. With a yank of her hand, the mother pulled Qiu Ru back. For a time, the lieutenant looked over the group, seeing that no one else was liable to interrupt, before he looked at Chief Tan.

"Tan Fu, Qiu Lee, Long Mao. Join the others," Chief Tan said softly.

Everyone knew why he had chosen the three, of course. Their families had been gifted with more than three surviving sons. Even now, their parents would have a single son left to work the farm, turn the earth. A good thing. Better than the families that were left without any. If you didn't consider the fact that now, three of their sons were fighting a war that none of them ever wanted.

"Good," the lieutenant said as his gaze slid over the new conscripts.

Wu Ying looked to the side as well, offering Fa Hui a tight smile as he saw his big friend look sallow and scared.

"Conscripts, return to your homes and collect your belongings. You will not be back for many months. Bring what you need. We will march in fifteen minutes. Gather at first bell," the lieutenant said.

The students stared at one another, looking at the few members of the class that were left, then at the other children. Wu Ying sighed and clapped Fa Hui on the shoulder, giving the giant a slight shove to send him toward his family. As if the motion was a signal, the group broke apart, the teenager's faces fixed as they moved to say their final goodbyes.

Read more of *A Thousand Li: the First Step*

https://starlitpublishing.com/products/the -first-step

Author's Note

When I was invited to the Action Fantasy Book Club, I debated putting a book free for it or taking the opportunity to write a work on a character I'd wanted to explore for a bit.

Obviously, I chose to write it, and the Sundering Blade exploring Master Cheng, Long Wu Ying's (the protagonist of my series A Thousand Li) enigmatic mentor, was born.

There are some differences. Master Cheng in the books is less pretentious, less stuck up. The experiences in this book and in the future shaves some off his arrogance off, but this sets up much of the conflict we see in the next six books.

I hope you enjoyed this work and the world I've built. If you do, I'd recommend reading *A Thousand Li: the First Step* that is both a more gradual introduction to the magic system involved and also the world at large.

~Tao

Want to chat *A Thousand Li* with other readers? Join the Tao Wong Author Group on Facebook to talk about my books, receive exclusive updates, and take part in exciting giveaways:
https://www.facebook.com/groups/taowongauthorgroup

About the Author

Tao Wong is a Canadian author based in Toronto who is best known for his System Apocalypse post-apocalyptic LitRPG series and A Thousand Li, a Chinese xianxia fantasy series. His work has been released in audio, paperback, hardcover and ebook formats and translated into German, Spanish, Portuguese, Russian and other languages. He was shortlisted for the UK Kindle Storyteller award in 2021 for his work, A Thousand Li: the Second Sect. When he's not writing and working, he's practicing martial arts, reading and dreaming up new worlds.

Tao became a full-time author in 2019 and is a member of the Science Fiction and Fantasy Writers of America (SFWA) and Novelists Inc.

If you'd like to support Tao directly, he has a Patreon page - benefits include previews of all his new books, full access to series short stories, and other exclusive perks:

http://www.patreon.com/taowong

Want updates on upcoming deluxe editions and exclusive merch? Follow Tao on Kickstarter to get notifications on all projects:

https://www.kickstarter.com/profil e/starlitpublishing

For updates on the series and his other books (and special one-shot stories), please visit the author's website: http://www.mylifemytao.com/

Subscribers to Tao's mailing list to receive exclusive access to short stories in the Thousand Li and System Apocalypse universes.

For more great information about great LitRPG series, check out the Facebook groups:

- GameLit Society

  https://www.facebook.com/groups/LitRPGsociety/

- LitRPG Books

  https://www.facebook.com/groups/LitRPG.books/

And join Tao Wong's Cultivation Novel Group for more recommendations and to talk about the Thousand Li series:

https://www.facebook.com/groups/cultivationnovels/

About the Publisher

Starlit Publishing is wholly owned and operated by Tao Wong. It is a science fiction and fantasy publisher focused on the LitRPG & cultivation genres. Their focus is on promoting new, upcoming authors in the genre whose writing challenges the existing stereotypes while giving a rip-roaring good read.

For more information on Starlit Publishing, early access to books and exclusive stories visit our webshop: https://www.starlitpublishing.com/

You can also join Starlit Publishing's mailing list to learn of new, exciting authors and book releases!

9 781778 551246